QUANAH

Made by the same Great Spirit, and living in the same land with our brothers, the red men, we consider ourselves as of the same family; we wish to live with them as one people, and to cherish their interests as our own.

Thomas Jefferson

QUANAH
The Serpent Eagle

by Paul Foreman

NORTHLAND PRESS  FLAGSTAFF, ARIZONA

*To LaDonna and Fred Harris,
their faith and their hope*

The publishers gratefully acknowledge the cooperation of the following institutions and their permission to reproduce their material: The Smithsonian Institution, pages ii, 72, 74, 76, 77, 78; the University of Oklahoma Press, page 73; and Doubleday and Company, page 75.

FRONTISPIECE

Quanah Parker, last free war and medicine chief of the Comanche Indians. Courtesy, Smithsonian Institution, Bureau of American Ethnology

Copyright © 1983 by Paul Foreman
All Rights Reserved
FIRST EDITION
ISBN 0-87358-324-8 softcover
ISBN 0-87358-329-9 hardcover

Library of Congress Catalog Card Number 82-62545
Composed and Printed in the United States of America

CONTENTS

PROLOGUE	1
Chapter One PEASE RIVER, 1860	5
Chapter Two RED RIVER	9
Chapter Three PARKER'S FORT, NAVASOTA RIVER	11
Chapter Four PARKER'S FORT	13
Chapter Five CLEAR FORK OF THE BRAZOS RIVER	15
Chapter Six THE FALLS OF THE CLEAR FORK	17
Chapter Seven FORT SMITH, ARKANSAS	21
Chapter Eight TEHUACANA HILL	24
Chapter Nine PARKER'S FORT	27
Chapter Ten NAVASOTA RIVER	30
Chapter Eleven PRICKLY ASH AND PEYOTE	32
Chapter Twelve CLEAR FORK OF THE BRAZOS	37
Chapter Thirteen COMANCHE PEAK	41
Chapter Fourteen BOSQUE RIVER	48

Chapter Fifteen	PALO DURO CANYON	51
Chapter Sixteen	FORT CONCHO	54
Chapter Seventeen	CONCHOS RIVER	57
Chapter Eighteen	CONCHOS RIVER WALK	64
Chapter Nineteen	THE WHITE RIVER	67
Chapter Twenty	A LEATHER QUIRT	69
Chapter Twenty-One	CHISOS MOUNTAINS	79
Chapter Twenty-Two	MESCALERO APACHE	84
Chapter Twenty-Three	THE WAGON RAID	87
Chapter Twenty-Four	DOUBLE MOUNTAIN	91
Chapter Twenty-Five	MEDICINE CHIEF	96
Chapter Twenty-Six	ISHTAI'S MEDICINE	99
Chapter Twenty-Seven	ADOBE WALLS	102
Chapter Twenty-Eight	ISHTAI'S LAST MEDICINE	114
Chapter Twenty-Nine	BUFFALO WALLOW	117
Chapter Thirty	FORT SILL	123
Chapter Thirty-One	FATHER PEYOTE	126
Chapter Thirty-Two	TWO DIFFERENT PATHS	128
Chapter Thirty-Three	PALO DURO CANYON	132
Chapter Thirty-Four	MACKENZIE'S PUDDING	140
Chapter Thirty-Five	CANADIAN RIVER	142
Chapter Thirty-Six	FORT SILL, 1875	145
EPILOGUE		149
PHOTOGRAPHS		71

This is a work of fiction based on an historical person. It is an attempt to imagine the last days of the Comanche as a free people through the eyes of one of their leaders. Those who are heirs to the oral tradition will best judge how closely I come to the spirit of Quanah, the Serpent Eagle.

PAUL FOREMAN

PROLOGUE

Some six hundred years ago, the Comanches, as part of a larger series of migrations, left their ancient homeland in Idaho. They traveled up the Snake River, down the eastern slopes of the Rockies, and onto the high plains the Spanish called the *Llano Estacado*—land so flat that, later, the conquistadores could only cross by following the stakes of yucca stalks planted by the Comanches.

Near the headwaters of the Rio Grande, the Comanches, who called themselves Paducahs or Numernah, traded or stole horses from the Spanish and developed a horse culture, becoming perhaps the greatest horsemen of the Native American tribes.

Three centuries before, their close kinsmen, the Aztec, built *Tenochtitlan* and conquered all of Mexico. The Comanches, with the horses they tamed and bred, conquered a large area the Spanish called the *Comancheria*. It stretched from the Arkansas River on the north to the edge of the Edwards Plateau in south Texas—at times on to the Rio Grande—and from the Pecos River on the west to as far east into the cross timbers as they wanted to ride, often as far as the Sabine River.

Great rivers drained the caprock of the southern plains into Oklahoma and Texas: the Canadian, the Red River, the Trinity, the Brazos, and the Colorado. These marked their special hunting

The Comanche, with the horses they trained and bred, came to conquer a large area [that was] called the Comancheria. The horse was the key to Comanche power. Their almost mystical attachment to and control over the animal gave them the vehicle to cross the immensity of Texas like the wind that blew so fiercely across the Staked Plains. The Comanches were feared by neighboring tribes; their cunning, skill, and daring were admired, even by the United States Army, their avowed enemy. Their horses were like straws in the wind that fed the power of the Quohadi [Comanche].

grounds. Other tribes—the Apache, Tonkawa, Jumano—stood against them, but briefly. To the vast Pueblo settlements of New Mexico, the Comanches were such fierce enemies that the Pueblo children called everyone and everything in the east "Comanche."

In the late eighteenth century, the Spanish tried to settle the southern part of the Comanche domain. A few missions, like San Antonio and Goliad, survived. Others, such as San Saba, despite its riches in silver, did not. In the early 1820s, Moses Austin and his son, Stephen F. Austin, led colonies of Virginians into this new land called Texas. Thomas Jefferson encouraged Moses Austin in his efforts, and the earliest Saxon colonists included such Virginia names as Dabney and Wythe.

They converted to Catholicism; many married Spanish wives. They generally kept first, the Spanish law, and later, the Mexican Constitution. In 1836, these new Saxon *Texanos* rose against the dictator, Santa Anna, and took the province of Texas from Mexico, establishing the Lone Star Republic. The thick limestone walls of the Alamo that had protected the Spanish padres against the Comanches, sheltered Crockett and Travis for much of their seige.

The first president of the Republic of Texas, the hero of San Jacinto, Sam Houston, had a wise and just policy towards the Indians of Texas. He had lived thirteen years with the Cherokees and respected Indian ways. His successor, Mirabeau B. Lamar, was a disaster; his only policy towards the Indians was that of eradication. Only against the weaker coastal tribes did Lamar prevail; against the Comanches, he failed. The Comanches ruled the southern plains until the 1870s when the main events of this story took place.

It would be impossible to tell the whole story of the Comanches. Here, we are concerned only with Quanah, the last chief of the Comanches. His mother was Cynthia Ann Parker, whose story was legend on the frontier. In the 1830s, a band of Predestinarian Baptists, led by their elders, settled in the Robertson Colony near the Navasota River. This settlement was close to the present town of Mexia, which was named for the Mexican General who changed sides and fought for Houston in the War for Independence.

After Texas gained its severance from Mexico, a large band of Comanches made a raid on Parker's Fort. Most of the men were away in the fields, and the Comanches slew and mutilated the men who remained in the fort, raped the women before they killed them, and carried the children away into captivity—including Cynthia Ann, a girl of seven or eight.

Years later, when Texas joined the United States, the U.S. Army met with nearly all the Comanche tribes at Comanche Peak, a flat plateau in Hood County just west of the Brazos, near what is now called Granbury. Their purpose was to tell the Comanches they were Americans and under the rule of the Great White Father in Washington. The Comanches waited for two or three months for the army to find the flat-topped, arrowhead-shaped mound, and had many marriages and feasts while they waited. The heavily wooded slopes of the peak and the nearby river bottom were full of deer, bear, buffalo, wild turkey, and other game.

We can imagine that Cynthia Ann, whose Comanche name was Naduah, married the great chief, Peta Noconah, during this festival summer. Or it may have been on this flat-topped mountain where Quanah was conceived or born. A hundred years after the Comanches were officially added to the American nation, young boys still found arrowheads, broad hunting points as well as more slender war points, in the fields around Comanche Peak. The boys asked their fathers about the red man who had inhabited this land for so long. As boys themselves, the fathers had heard stories from the men who had fought the Comanches, and their replies would center on the last great representative of his people, the man called Quanah Parker. His name is well known to history, and the years he led the Comanche in their last free wanderings on the plains are now legend. This, then, is the story of Quanah, the serpent eagle of the Comanche nation.

CHAPTER I PEASE RIVER, 1860

The sun broke the brittle quiet of the cold winter darkness on the northern Texas plains. The wind, which had blown all night, dropped off. The solid bank of low-slung clouds shivered and cracked before the spreading dawn.

Quanah rubbed his eyes and reached for his moccasins. His father, Noconah, was already out with a hunting party, stalking the young buck deer before they bedded down in the breaks. How long would it be until he trained his senses to wake before first light so he might join them on the hunt? Today, as yesterday and the one before, he would have to hunt alone.

His mother, Naduah, handed him two large slices of buffalo meat she had warmed at the fire. There was no need to speak. The love that shone in her eyes for her tall handsome son of fourteen years negated the need for idle words. Topsanah, his baby sister, was awake now and made low moans for her morning feeding. Naduah unfolded her antelope dress and lifted the child up to her breast. Quanah never ceased to marvel at the milky whiteness of her underbreasts and the bright red nipples. No other women in the tribe had these colors. The Quohadi band of Comanches stayed on the high plains and seldom crossed paths with white men. The thought flashed through his mind that his father must be a great chief to have so many horses and a wife of such beauty."

He gathered up his cedar bow, his willow arrows, flint knife, and pouch of flints and loose keepstones, and spoke. "I go."

"*Hai*, go, my son, and bring me a rabbit for my pot." She returned to rocking and crooning her baby. Topsanah crooned back, her lips never slacking in their strong, steady suck.

Quanah quietly stole from the camp. There were no other boys near his age. Those just older were hunting with the men. The younger ones were much shorter than he, and, bothered by some of his strange ways, would taunt him about his name. *Quanah* can mean a big stink, like the spray of a polecat. Quanah knew, too, that his name meant *eagle*, but as yet he had no eagle feather for his braids, nor would he wear one until his namedream and subsequent deeds allowed him to do so.

Up on the banks above the river, the trees thinned into prairie; there he would find his rabbits. It was cold even for midwinter, but the wind was still and Quanah felt the sun's warmth slowly begin to thaw the air.

The brown fur of a cottontail caught his eye. He nocked an arrow in his bow and slowly stalked his prey. He moved so quietly and imperceptibly that the rabbit, even though it saw him, was unafraid. Keeping his bow on a flat plane with his waist, Quanah slowly drew it taut as his father taught him. The arrow flew. The cottontail jumped in the air, then crumpled on the frozen ground, its lifeblood flowing from the edge of the shaft in its side. Quanah exulted within, but made no sound as he took his flint knife and gutted the rabbit and stuck it on his willow pole.

He was sure he saw another one about a hundred yards ahead, back toward the river. Walking slowly in a crouch, another arrow at the ready, he trod so lightly that the sound of his feet crunching on the frozen ground barely reached even his own ears.

Perhaps because he was so quiet inside, with the stillness of the hunt, he was able to hear the drumming of many horses while they were yet out of sight. Horses? Or buffalo? Far too many for his father's hunting party. Darting past the rabbit, Quanah gained the cover of the woods and dropped, panting, into a shallow gully filled with driftwood. Up on the hill rose a sight he had never seen before.

Sul Ross and his band of sixty rangers, armed to the teeth, had been riding for two weeks with no sign of the Comanches who had made the devastating raids along the Brazos above Waco in late November. They waited until Christmas before starting out. Now, in the middle of January, they saw the tepees and smoking campfires of the Comanche along the Pease River, more than two hundred miles north of where they began their search. No way to tell if these were the Indians who had made the raid, and no need for discernment. His men wanted blood, as did he. Now they would have it.

The horsemen stretched their mounts out from a fast trot into a full gallop as they unlimbered their rifles. It was January, 1860; in another year they would be gone to fight with Jackson and Lee in the Civil War. But now, the *Co-man-che*, the bald and wise ones, were the enemy. Abraham Lincoln was but a dreaded and feared whisper.

Quanah peered over the rim of the gully and watched as the shaggy-bearded white men poured down like hailstones upon his tribe. Only a few old men were left in the camp. The handful of them who fought, one with a lance, two with flint hatchets, were shot down. The tepees were razed, some catching fire. The Quohadi women and children fled like quail up and down the river. Some rangers, their fingers numb from resting so long on their triggers and their judgment equally numb, shot and killed the women who were slow to flee. Sul Ross, a giant of a man, swung the flat of his sword at the head of a young Comanche woman; as the blade fell, she turned her head to see who pursued her, and the sharp steel sliced quickly into her jugular vein. She died in seconds on the icy ground. Ross and his great Morgan stallion rode on; his sword rose and fell twice more, no longer turned flat. The heat of the spurting Comanche blood generated a raging fire in his chest.

Another ranger, Lidbury, overtook a Comanche woman clutching a small child. She stumbled and fell. As he raised his rifle to shoot her, he was stunned by the flash of blue eyes in the deeply tanned face. "My god, a white woman! . . . Who are you? What's your name? Your name?"

The words, sharp as mesquite thorns, sank deeply into her. She had not heard her native speech in twenty years. Out of an unponderable depth of memory and dire necessity, she mumbled, "M-m-m . . . me! Me, Cynthia."

Lidbury knew at once who she must be—Cynthia Ann Parker, captured as a young girl by the Comanches in the terrible raid on Parker's Fort at Mexia. He gently lowered his rifle. "Don't worry! I won't shoot. You're okay. I ain't gonna shoot you. You're with your own kind now."

He began to realize she didn't understand him very well, but the steady tone of his voice was slowly reassuring her. The fear of death had gone from her eyes, only to be replaced by a new apprehension. With his lowered barrel, he motioned her to go in front of him back to the campgrounds, where Ross and his rangers were regrouping to gloat over their victory.

Ross spoke loudly to his men. "You've done it, men. We've made short work of these Comanches. They won't be stealing horses for a while!" A coarse, ragged laughter ran through the rangers.

"But most of their warriors are gone, likely on a hunting party. We'll head straight south and drop off these two dozen squaws and littl'uns at the reservation on the Clear Fork of the Brazos. Not likely we'll be attacked so long as we've got these hostages. Lidbury, what have you got there?"

"Captain, it's a white woman. Look at them eyes. Blue as a bluebonnet, or my name is Sunday! And if I ain't mistaken, she might be Cynthia Ann Parker!"

CHAPTER II   RED RIVER

Quanah's legs ached; his hands hung limp at his sides. Now, after the battle of Pease River, he was leading the handful who hadn't been captured toward the big Comanche campground on the Red River.

In addition to himself, there were three younger children, including his little brother Pecos, and five of the youngest Comanche wives who had fled on fleet legs from the wrath of the rangers. Where his father and the band of Quohadi hunters were, he had no idea; he could not see them with his inner eye.

Quanah meant eagle, the far-seeing lord of the skies. Pecos meant fish, the life that quickens the rivers. Yet here, he and his brother were running like rabbits before the angry hawk-nosed rangers. *Tejanos,* they were called by the Mexican traders from Santa Fe. Quanah worried most for his mother, he had seen the man nearly kill her before capturing her. What fate waited her at their hands, and his little sister, Topsanah, the prairie flower, who still sucked at the breast and could not even walk?

Now they could sight the fires of the camp. The woods were thicker as the plains broke down toward the Red River valley. Many campfires lifted their smoke above the willows, cottonwoods, and pecans. Horse Back, the great chief of all the Comanches, who had led the war party on the *Tejanos* after the treachery in the Council

House at San Antonio, would be in camp. Noconah had told him there were none braver or swifter in battle than Horse Back.

These were *Coth-cho-tekas*, the buffalo clan that often hunted with the antelope clan. Surely their brothers in the buffalo clan would take them into their lodges now in the dead of winter. Especially after he gave his report to Horse Back. At the thought of facing the great chief, his heart trembled in his chest, but his face grew more set and stern.

The cry went up in the camp as the small band approached. The buffalo clan women sent up wailing cries as if it had been their own men who had been slain. Quanah, who was perceived as their leader, though he was but a tall, strong boy, was led into Horse Back's tent to tell the great chief of the misfortune that had befallen his clan.

Quanah stood still and steady before the formidable chief, though his heart was thumping loudly inside his chest. He kept telling it to be quiet lest Horse Back should hear. Horse Back instructed Quanah to sit down, in kind, quick tones that told Quanah that he was in the best and wisest of hands.

"Now, tell me, young Quanah, what has happened. Though I have not seen you in many moons, I know you. You have the nose of your mother, Naduah, and the brow of your father, Noconah. Tell me this great trouble which brings you here."

"Oh great chief Horse Back, the white men—the *Tejanos*—came when the men were away. They killed all the old men still in the village, and many of the women. They took many captive, and led them away with ropes tied around their necks. Naduah, my mother, they took. The few of us who escaped, I led here. I knew what little we could do in the face of so many guns, and we had no horses. I knew Horse Back would know what was best."

"You did well, young Quanah. You are a leader like your father. He, too, I fear for. The hunting warriors, when they return, will trail after the raiding party to try and bring their wives home. We may never see them again. Until your father returns, Quanah, you will stay here in my tent, you and young Pecos. I will throw my blanket over you. Now, go and tell the others. Horse Back will talk with the spirits. The spirits will tell what has befallen the parents of young Quanah."

CHAPTER III   PARKER'S FORT, NAVASOTA RIVER

Cynthia looked at the plate of food in front of her. There were pinto beans, turnip greens, cornbread, a thick, almost rancid slab of old pork, and a small dab of cane syrup for sweetener. She knew she needed better food. Her milk was very thin, and less of it filled her breasts now. Her baby daughter had grown sick and barely had strength to pull the milk down. The Comanches ate better meat, daily. So, she began to tell her white brothers, Red and John Parker, about her oldest son, Quanah. She sensed that her beloved husband, Noconah, had entered the spirit world. If only Quanah were here, he would bring her fresh meat.

Quanah lay rolled up in the buffalo robe in Horse Back's lodge, unable to sleep. He could not quite enter the spirit world of dreams, either. Before all this happened, and his mother and father were swept away by the violent wind from the south, he could stay awake at the verge of sleep and enter the spirit world voluntarily. He saw many things there: the deer and the buffalo, the rivers and creeks he knew, the colors of the light-scented willows, and the deep green of the pecan trees. Even now, he could remember some of what he had seen in the spirit world the night before. This helped the turbulence to subside, and the gate of his mind swung open. His soul flew like a young eagle into the realms of night searching for his lost parents.

Noconah was nowhere to be found. Quanah could feel him, but not see him. It was as if a high bluff, like the walls of the Palo Duro Canyon, stood between him and his father, and he could not rise above the walls. He could see his mother, though. A sad, heavy frown lay on her brow. Her lips opened as if to call his name. "Quanah! Quanah!"

There was a fire behind her. He saw the glow briefly kindle in her red-blonde hair, then lost her in the coils of sleep.

CHAPTER IV — PARKER'S FORT

The long wail of the Comanche death-chant rose again and again within the rough-walled log house. Cynthia Ann's daughter, Prairie Flower, had passed into the beyond. She knew, too, that the little one was only following the great Noconah, who so often would come home laughing, a deer slung about his shoulders. She felt she must soon enter that long dark cave herself, to search for her loved ones. If only she could see her beloved Quanah.

Red and John Parker stood and talked in troubled whispers under the huge spreading post oak that dominated the center of their compound. "What can we do for her, John? She won't let anyone touch that dead baby."

"Just wait her out. She's been through a lot of grief. She may sense we're her kin, but she only knew us when she was mighty small. She is a Comanche through and through. I think she will come back to us. Just give her time."

"Do you reckon we ought to go look for that boy of hers, that Quanah she keeps talking about?"

"We might, in the spring. That could ease her lot, but it would make ours harder. Then we would have two Comanches under our roof. Don't get me wrong. I am glad we got her back, but she sure is a strange and wild one. I suspect I would be, too, if I had lived out there on the plains with the Comanches."

Within a few short weeks Cynthia Ann Parker, the beloved Naduah to the Comanches, died. She shoved away most of the food and water her brothers and their wives brought. She let them take the dead child and bury it, but she wouldn't budge from her spot. One night, under a full moon, Red Parker woke to hear her lightly singing her own death song. The song was strange to his ears, and he didn't know what it meant, but it somehow fit in with the eerie, ghostlike quality of the moonlight that washed the Texas land. In the morning she was dead, and Red understood the sad tones of the song she had been singing.

The ground was still hard with winter as they buried her under the great old post oak, not fifty steps from the spot where she had been taken that bright October morning, twenty-five years before.

"The Lord gives. The Lord takes away. Blessed be the name of the Lord. We commend unto you our sister, O Lord. Her life has been short and full of woe. Give her a home with thee and give her rest. This we humbly plead in Jesus' name. Amen."

In the spring, Red and John Parker left their homes and families and headed up on the high plains to seek and find Quanah Parker. It was a painfully familiar quest; for each of seventeen years they had set out on a similar mission: their sister, Cynthia Ann, the object.

CHAPTER V   CLEAR FORK OF THE BRAZOS RIVER

Quanah sat near the stream in the willows, whittling arrows with his flint knife. The Clear Fork of the Brazos wasn't clear, but at least the water was sweet. It didn't leave one thirstier, like a swallow from the Salt Fork would. Now and then, when his mouth dried from his efforts, Quanah would dip a hand down into the river and carry the good water to his mouth.

Quanah was still deeply troubled by his dream of the night before. It seemed he could hear his father's voice calling him, but he could never see Noconah's face. He had awakened sharply from the dream, but saw only Horse Back and his three wives in a deep sleep, snoring peacefully.

That morning, he had asked Horse Back about the spirit world, and how those who had gone there would come back, if ever. At first Horse Back was reluctant to talk, but when he saw Quanah would not be satisfied without an answer, he spoke.

"Quanah, the spirits of our fathers can always speak to us. We cannot always speak to them. To have the namedream, one must go without food and water, and sit and meditate in one of the holy spots—the four sisters, our medicine mounds, the buffalo mound of Tolopah, or the spreading eagle mound on this river. Then, when the head opens to hear the voices of the upper world, the fathers who named you send your medicine sign, the animal who holds your strength and wisdom. He comes and shows his light in your face.

"Sometimes, at such moments, the old ones come and show their faces, too. Often they come as buffalo, or antelope, running in great herds. Most rarely do they come as the great gray wolf, the *doucah* of our people, or his lesser brother, the sly coyote. Only the greatest chiefs have ever seen the wolf in their namedreams."

"Did you see the wolf, mighty Horse Back?"

"Yes, Quanah, yes. Even rarer still is the snake, the oldest sign of our people. The snake will often come in an ordinary dream, but almost never in a namedream. The snake, the wolf, the eagle—none has cunning like these. The sign of our people is the snake wriggling backwards, which tells the story of our ancient homeland and the great migrations. The eagle clutching the snake, which you see on my shield, shows the great spirit reaching down from the upper air and seizing his people, lifting them up to behold their destiny.

"We must always follow the voice of the great spirit that calls, even here, within our chest. But first, we must hear him. Your father, Noconah, your mother, Naduah, and your sister, Topsanah, are within his hands. He has not left them without a comforter. Soon, Quanah, you will go up on the mountain and talk with the spirits of your fathers."

CHAPTER VI THE FALLS OF THE CLEAR FORK

Red and John Parker had ridden far; their horses were wet and tired. They were headed toward the falls on the Clear Fork of the Brazos, where the trader, Barnard, had told them they would find the Comanche chief Horse Back at this time of year.

Barnard had been there on the flat roof of Comanche Peak in 1846 when the American soldiers gave the declaration to the Comanches telling them they were now under the protection of the Great White Father in Washington. He had met Horse Back then and had set up his trading post at Chalk Mountain in the shadow of Comanche Peak—the first one west of the Brazos. He had been friends of Horse Back and the buffalo clan ever since; small wonder, for he was their sole source of tobacco.

Red pulled his wide-brimmed hat down to shade his eyes against the late afternoon sun. It had been four days since they left Barnard; surely they would hit the Clear Fork soon. Their water was low, and here on the higher plains the creeks were fewer and farther between.

When they saw it, their hearts lifted. The dark, low line of trees was made up of scrub oak, cottonwood, and pecan. Their horses needed no prodding; at the scent of water they picked their gait up into a steady trot.

John had a few misgivings. "Red, you reckon we can just ride into that Comanche camp like nobody's business? I remember our promise to Cynthia Ann, but I need this wool on my head to keep my ears warm."

"Well, they've seen us by now. The Comanches will always see you well before you see them out here on these plains. Their eyes are trained to it and ours aren't. If Barnard is right, and we've no cause to doubt him, this crooked staff will tell them we come in peace."

From the line of antelope and buffalo skin tepees stretched along the river, they saw a small party of horsemen gather and ride toward them. The fear they felt was fear they dared not show; slowing their gait, they rode straight for the Comanche braves.

They were soon surrounded by fierce, well-armed horsemen, who directed them toward the center of the camp. There, an old man stood impassively, wearing a single eagle feather in his graying hair and a necklace of bear claws adorning his bare chest. From Barnard's description, Red recognized Chief Horse Back and spoke to him in the few Comanche words Barnard had taught him to say.

"Horse Back, Great Chief, wise in the ways of men and horses, hear us. We come in peace."

Horse Back was flattered at the Comanche words, poorly spoken as they were. With gestures, he motioned the Parkers down from their horses, squatted into a crosslegged seat on the ground, and signed them to do likewise.

Red Parker took the lead. Using key words he had learned from Barnard, he explained to Horse Back very slowly that they were brothers of Naduah, wife of Noconah.

At these names Horse Back perked up. These were no ordinary guests. He stood up, invited them into his lodge, and, like a chief, abruptly entered before them. Horse Back signalled them to take seats around the small bed of coals in the campfire, which still sent a spiral of smoke upwards. He called for his wife to bring the men some of the thick smoked buffalo steaks she had been preparing all day. Then he eased back and slowly and carefully fired up tobacco in his long-stemmed pipe made from red Siouxland pipestone. Once the pipe was going, he passed it to the Parkers and to Lone Wolf and Otter Belt, the two other chiefs who had joined him in the tent.

Red and John ate their steaks silently. There was a strong healthy bite to the buffalo meat, and the pungent aroma of the aged tobacco added to the meal. They knew Horse Back would talk when he was ready and not before. Horse Back's wife glided in and out of the circle like a shadow, handing more steaks to the hungry men.

At last, Horse Back drew long on his pipe as if to still his thinking, then spoke. "Tell me of my old friend, Barnard. Does his hair still warm his ears in the shadow of the holy mountain?"

Red answered slowly, mixing his English with what little Comanche he knew. "Barnard sends you his greetings. He also sends you this fresh tobacco I have here in my pouch." Red handed the oilskin-wrapped packet to Horse Back.

Horse Back leaned forward quickly, undid the package, knocked the fire out of the pipe, and carefully started filling the pipe with the fresher tobacco. "Tobacco sometimes grows too old, just like horses. New tobacco tastes sweeter. Tell Barnard Horse Back is very happy Barnard remembers him." They smoked in silence a few minutes more.

Then Horse Back started ruminating, almost as if the Parkers weren't there. "Yes, Lone Wolf, these are the brothers of our blessed Naduah. I can see her in their faces. The firelight does not lie. How many moons ago did she first appear among our people? Yes, I remember the day Peta Noconah took her to wife. It was during that summer the bluecoats met us on the great buffalo mountain to tell us Texas had joined with the lodges of the Great White Father in the east. Many a happy marriage that summer. The Comanches set aside their usual pursuits; we let the Tonkawa, the Waco, and the Apache go in peace like the porcupine. We spent the whole summer telling stories, wedding our sons and daughters, and waiting for the bluecoats to come and tell us we were 'Americans.'

"Now the Texans make war against the Great White Father. And they make war on the Comanches, too. When the Texans, the ones they call the 'Rangers,' came north two winters ago, like a whirlwind they swept away Noconah, his beautiful Naduah, her daughter Topsanah, and many another one. Now you come, wishing to take her son, Quanah, away with you."

Red and John looked startled as Horse Back guessed their motives. "Do not be surprised. Horse Back has spent many long years looking into the hearts of men. Your faces are open and honest. I should be surprised if I did not read what is written there. Yes, you may take Quanah. But not because you say it, and not because Horse Back speaks it. Naduah, from beyond the land of shadows, tells me this must happen. It is the way of the Comanche, that when a young man not yet a warrior, loses his father and mother, the brothers of his mother must rule his spirit until he has a name-dream. Otter Belt, go bring Quanah." Horse Back was careful not to mention Pecos, since he sensed the Parkers, for some reason, did not know of him. Horse Back wanted to keep one of Noconah's sons in his own lodge to train as a warrior.

Quanah's heart was low indeed as he rode from the Comanche camp that morning. His face was turned toward the earth. His ears burned as his playmates ran after his horse calling the name, "Qua-nah!" with the special tone that meant the stink of the striped skunk. Yet he dared not disobey Horse Back. Besides, he, too, could see his mother's face in the faces of these men, and they were kind like his mother. He also knew that the Great Spirit was testing him, stretching his heart tight like a hide over the drum of his ribs, to see if it might break.

Hours later, they stopped their horses under a small cluster of post oaks that broke the heat of the noonday sun. Quanah gladly wolfed down the jerky Red gave him and took long draughts of the sweet river water out of his antelope flask. His spirits picked up as he heard the low call of the mourning doves. The Great Spirit was near and no longer stretching him. Red and John Parker smiled to see the boy's eyes open. They were headed home, and Quanah was coming with them.

CHAPTER VII — FORT SMITH, ARKANSAS

Robert E. Lee finally surrendered the Confederate army in 1866 at Appomattox Courthouse. Ulysses S. Grant, deeply moved by the spirit of his now-defeated enemy, would not take Lee's sword. The Union, though drained of blood from every farmstead, held, though the true architect of the North's victory, Abraham Lincoln, lay in his tomb at Springfield.

Congress was restless; peace brought more uncertainties than war. Would the South rise again? No chances were taken. The mighty Union army fanned out over the South to occupy and drive home the defeat. The old Indian forts on the southwest border—Fort Smith, Fort Sill, Fort Richardson—were reoccupied.

Confederate soldiers, most of them walking by now, turned homeward. Often their womenfolk had not heard from them for months and years; they would see them coming up the road like gray and grimly behaunted ghosts out of the past. Many who returned to Texas found their homesteads abandoned due to Indian depredations, or met stories of hardship equal to the ones they had known in Tennessee or the wilderness of Virginia.

Confederate soldiers returning to their farms and plantations in Georgia, Mississippi, and Alabama, as well as Virginia and Tennessee, often found their slaves gone, their stock eaten or abandoned, and their outbuildings and barns burned, and sometimes their houses burned as well. Many lingered only long enough to build a wagon, trade their ruined farms for horses and supplies, pack up their families, and head for Texas and the promise of new land and a new start.

At Fort Smith, General William Tecumseh Sherman was briefing the officers who would command the frontier forts. There was Nelson Miles, Ranald Mackenzie, and General Phil Sheridan, all with outstanding records in the late War of the Rebellion.

Sherman alternately stroked his short beard and ran his hand over his balding pate as he spoke. "Men, while the war was going on, the Indian situation on the frontier went to hell. Red Cloud up in the Dakotas and Iowa is running circles around Kearny. Black Kettle and the southern Cheyenne are holding war councils and sun dances. The Comanche and Kiowa are raiding clear across Texas, and the Osage varmints are stealing cows and horses right beneath our noses.

"On top of that, we've got dozens of Quaker missionaries descending on the reservations; they say the red man is basically good, just poorly understood; hell, the only *good* Indian is a *dead* Indian!

"So, until we get the go-ahead from Washington, which isn't likely until '68, when old Ulysses gets in the White House and gives us our marching orders—well, until then, we'll just fight a holding action. Miles, you'll be in the thick of it at Fort Sill where the Kiowa and Comanche and Osage are on the reservation. As soon as we can, we'll move the Comanche up there, off the Clear Fork of the Brazos. Mackenzie, I'm putting you on point. You'll be at Fort Concho right in the middle of the Comanche raiding route. On your way down, I want you to go by the old fort on the Navasota River called Parker's Fort. Those Parkers have been bedeviled by the Comanche for thirty years. You'll find out something there. Phil Sheridan will command at Fort Smith and be in charge of the whole area south of the Platte. I'll be on the frontier as often as I can when I'm not talking to those pettifogging jackanapes in bloomer britches back in Washington. Well, that will be all, gentlemen!"

Walking out the door, Mackenzie, an exceptionally handsome officer, fraternally clasped Miles by the elbow. "Nelson, I hear you're taking your new bride, Sarah, out to Indian Territory."

"That's right, Ranald. All the officers in my command will be bringing their wives to Fort Sill. I believe it will help the morale of the troops, given the unpleasantness of the duty."

"Just don't get so soft you let the Kiowas under Striking Eagle slide off the reservation."

"Don't you worry. Anyway, when you feel you need a touch of civilization, and you're tired of talking to Texans, white or red, come to see us at Fort Sill."

A broad smile flashed across Mackenzie's face as he limped along on his bad leg, which still carried a minié ball in the knee. "I'll surely take you up on that. Miles, you're my kind of man!"

As Mackenzie walked away, Miles pondered the meaning of what he had just said. Something about it troubled him. No matter. He'll be so busy chasing Comanches I'll never see him, nor will Sarah, he thought. Miles knew there had been something between them at West Point back before the war, where Sarah, the daughter of General Fox, had been the belle of every occasion. But Sarah had chosen him and waited for him. Then, too, perhaps Mackenzie had never played his hand. The last thought that snared Miles' mind was that he might be so busy chasing the Indians he would have no time for his beautiful and exuberant wife.

CHAPTER VIII   TEHUACANA HILL

Quanah was unhappy at Parker's Fort, though he tried hard to do what his uncles asked and expected of him. He hated sleeping inside the stockade; the air was stale in the tight little huts when he woke in the morning. He dreaded his morning chores, especially chopping wood with the axe he had not yet learned to handle. The wood groaned under the axe; when he used his flint knife to cut cedar bows and willow arrows, the wood scarcely whispered.

Red Parker could tell the boy was not happy, but he had an idea of how to improve the situation. That morning over flapjacks (after thirty days of flapjacks, Quanah was more than hungry for buffalo meat), Red spoke to John. "John, I heard from Abe Thomason that the band of Caddos camped over around Tehuacana Hill had some spotted horses they got in trade with the Comanches. I think I'll go trade for a couple, and set Quanah here to breaking them."

"Sounds good to me, Red. You want I should ride along?"

"No, I'll take Quanah on the mare, and young Silas can double up behind me on the roan. I'll take along some of that pretty calico—it will appeal to the old chief's eyes."

Quanah's spirits lifted once they were out of sight of the fort. When they waded their horses across the lovely Navasota River, he saw some large catfish swirl away into the green depths. They made him think of Pecos, his younger brother. He knew Pecos was free and safe in Horse Back's tent. He spoke under his breath in Comanche to the catfish, "*Hai*, Pecos!"

"What was that, Quanah?"

"Big fish, Uncle Red. You want, we wait, I catch."

"Naw, better not. We've got bigger fish to catch up yonder at Tehuacana Hill, some real Appaloosa ponies."

The Caddo camp was small and bustling. The children couldn't take their eyes off Quanah. Who was this Comanche who rode with the white man? He was Comanche sure enough—just look at his leggings; that light gray antelope hide came only from the high plains. The Caddo elders paid no mind to Quanah; they wanted to see what the big bearded white man named Parker had brought them. The white man was always bringing them something.

The Caddo squaws could barely withhold their delighted squeaks and giggles when they saw the pretty bolts of red and blue calico speckled with yellow and white flowers. Even the old chief grunted his approval. "Very fine, Big Parker! What you want for this? You want my wife yonder, you take!" He was just joking, but with the calico he could have gotten another wife, so it was more than just an idle jest.

"Nope! I want two of those six wild horses hobbled over there. Just two." He held up two fingers. "I bring you two bolts of cloth, keep you warm in winter."

"Those horses wild, Big Parker. Not even you can ride!"

Red smiled. He knew he had the chief now. "True, I could not ride them. This boy here is the son of my sister. His name is Quanah. He is Comanche, Quohadi Comanche. He can ride them. Do you want the cloth?"

The old chief smiled back; he liked to trade with Big Parker. "Yes, the Comanche and the horse were made for each other. Yes, your Comanche boy looks good, Big Parker. Yes, we will take the cloth now. Yes, you take the two horses you like best."

Quanah unlimbered the extra ropes they had brought along. He spoke, almost out of turn, "Uncle Red, you want me to pick them?"

"Yes, Quanah, you pick them."

Quanah went to the horses and ran his hands expertly over their backs and legs. He quickly slipped the ropes over the heads of two of them. Red could see that Quanah had made the best choices. He hadn't picked the biggest ones, but the best muscled, the ones that would have staying power.

The old Caddo chief, a leader of the Tejas tribe that had camped near Tehuacana Hill from time beyond memory, grunted approvingly. "Your Comanche boy, Big Parker—Quanah you call him—Quanah is true Comanche; he knows his horses."

CHAPTER IX   PARKER'S FORT

A few days later at Parker's Fort, there was a lot of commotion outside the gates. Colonel Ranald Mackenzie and his detachment of cavalry approached through the fields and the men and the boys, who had been harvesting the first crop of corn, accompanied him into the fort. They were the first Union soldiers young Silas Parker had seen, and he didn't think they looked too evil. His mother had told him to stay away from those "devil Yankees."

Inside the compound, Quanah was hard at work breaking the wild ponies. Each morning he would get on one of the horses and ride till it quit bucking. Neither horse had managed to throw him yet. Each morning the horses bucked a little bit less before they came to accept the strange, lithe weight on their backs.

As Mackenzie rode into the fort, Quanah gave the wild Appaloosa its head. The pony spun around and around, sunfished and sky-raked time and again. Slowly it spun down until it stood quaking like an aspen leaf. Quanah then gently nudged it with his knee into a short walk before sliding off and tying it up near the other pony, still lathered in sweat.

Calhoun, the sergeant who rode beside Mackenzie, muttered through his thick moustache and toothless gums, "That boy can ride, eh, Colonel!"

"That he can, Calhoun. These Indians are good for something. They can break horses or track game, but past that, they're worthless. Just crowbait, that's all."

Red Parker strode out of the main house in the enclosure to greet Mackenzie. "Howdy! You must be Colonel Mackenzie. We heard you might be coming our way. Won't you and your men sit a spell with us. We will have supper on shortly. I'm Red Parker, and this is my brother, John."

"Thank you, we are much obliged. Dismount! Calhoun, see to the horses, then meet me back here. I want to talk to these Parkers. I'm sure they can tell me something."

The Parkers gathered for the evening meal in their long house. The soldiers were amply provided with plates of pork and beans and bread in the grassy yard enclosed by the stockade.

When Mackenzie sat at the table, he saw real silverware alongside the bare wooden plates and knew the Parkers came from some older eastern family of lineage who treasured such things. Calhoun took a seat beside Mackenzie. The Parker men sat clustered at the head of the table of polished hand-hewn post oak, and the women sat around the foot. Opposite Mackenzie another place was set, still empty.

Calhoun and Mackenzie both were startled when the tall, eighteen-year-old Comanche boy they had seen breaking horses glided into the seat opposite and started helping himself to the beans and cornbread.

"I didn't know the Parkers sat to table with redskins." Mackenzie spoke in amazement.

Red Parker finished chewing his food before he replied. "That one there *is* a Parker, Colonel. That's Cynthia Ann's boy. His father was Peta Noconah, a great chief among the Comanches. That boy's parents are a lot better known in these parts than you. I ain't saying he's not a wild one. He may quit us and go back to the Comanches some day. But John and I traded with old Chief Horse Back when Cynthia Ann died, and Horse Back let him come with us. Seems like the Comanches respect the uncles on the mother's side most, when the parents are dead, and that applies whether they're red or white. So, as long as he stays, he eats with the rest of the Parkers."

Mackenzie took this gentle rebuke in silence. There was something at work here he didn't understand. Maybe the Parkers had lived too long on the frontier. Red Parker almost seemed to take more pride in the boy's Comanche blood lines than in the Parker side. This only added to the sensation that he, the Yankee Colonel, was an interloper here in a double sense: defending these ragged white Texans against the depredations of the Indians, for whom he had even less respect.

After a few moments of silence, Calhoun cleared his throat to speak. He had noticed the young Indian boy eyeing both him and Mackenzie very studiously and discreetly. He knew what pride the Comanches took in their names. He spoke, "Are you the one they call Quanah?"

Quanah straightened alertly, looked directly at Calhoun, and said distinctly in a low, untroubled voice, "Yes, I am Quanah."

Mackenzie, guessing Calhoun's game, and reasserting his authority, interrupted, "What does this name Quanah mean? Does it mean anything?"

Quanah looked in puzzlement at John Parker, the elder of the tribe of Predestinarian Baptists.

John gave the universal sign of the Comanche in sign language, the hand like a snake wriggling backwards. "Comanche—the snake wriggling backwards. Quanah—what does Quanah do?"

Quanah knit his brows for a moment. Then he spoke in his halting English. "Comanche boys say Quanah is a big stink, like the stink of the striped skunk. Noconah, Quanah's father, say Quanah is the eagle, the bird that comes out of the sun." Then Quanah's face became very animated, as if a new thread of consciousness was taking hold within him.

"Now, Quanah waddles on his belly through the grass like a skunk," and he walked his two fingers along the table, "but the day will come when Quanah will fly like the eagle in the sky." His hand shot upward with the fingers in an eloquent swoop above his head.

Mackenzie and Calhoun looked at the Indian boy, the Comanche Parker, with a newfound regard. They ate the rest of their meal in silence, thanked the Parkers, and bivouaced with their troops in the compound.

Quanah lay awake that night thinking about the bluecoat colonel. There was a certain fear in him, a quickness that darted like the head of a snake among the rocks.

CHAPTER X   NAVASOTA RIVER

The next morning the soldiers were gone. Neither the Parkers nor Quanah seemed to miss them. They were a new, unknown thread in the warp of Texas life. Some of the soldiers were Negroes with nappy hair; the Comanches called them buffalo soldiers.

After Quanah finished working with the horses that day, he tied them in the little corral in the corner of the huge stockade, leapt on his own speckled pony, and rode toward the nearby Navasota River to swim and fish. Quanah soon came to the deep, green hole of water with the gray limestone rocks embedded in one bank where the catfish loved to sleep.

He tied the horse to a low willow limb where it could eat the tender leaves, slipped his leggings and moccasins off, and dove naked into the clear river. Bursting from the surface, he swam by spinning around and around, then leaping almost entirely out of the water as he jackknifed and dove deep, touching the gravel bottom of the water hole. He looked not inhuman, but like a sleek brown otter as he plunged and capered by himself in the lazy, green river, drenched in the gold of the evening sunlight.

The snake doctors and dragonflies were lighting in the water; as Quanah paused in his cavorting, one lit on his nose. He held still to let the splash of its red wings wash over his eyes. He knew that many of these magic moments came to him from the Great Spirit, when his own spirit was free and ready for them. The grace of his freedom returned him sharply to the prison of his intentions, and he swam to the gray limestone rocks to dive for catfish. He knew that as long as he brought meat to their table, the Parkers would give him this freedom, this aloneness. After a few dives, he had four nice pan-size catfish strung on a willow stick.

One of the catfish finned him slightly on the hand when he made the first grab under the gillfins. He carefully washed the blood off in the creek, squeezed his hand to make it bleed again, then clamped it to his dry buckskins very tightly until the bleeding stopped. Quanah could not have told anyone where he had learned this; the knowledge that one washed a cut was in him. He also knew that no water was to be left in the cut when through.

After dressing, he mounted his pony and rode back to Parker's Fort, holding the fish out so their sharp gill fins would not rake his leg nor the pony.

He did not whistle. He did not sing. But deep within, a hum, steady as the drone of the bees and insects along the river, beat along his ribs.

CHAPTER XI PRICKLY ASH AND PEYOTE

The belly cramps came again, only this time more powerfully. Quanah staggered to his feet and pulled on his leggings. He must go to work in the corn fields with the others. This pain had been clawing at his guts for five days now. Each day he grew weaker. Stoically, he tried not to show the least discomfort.

As he reached the porch, Red Parker, standing nearby, mumbled aloud to his brother, John. "Say, Quanah sure looks under the weather." Even with one long, quick bound, he was not in time to catch Quanah as he crumpled in the dust, stricken with the weakness of his disease.

"What is it, boy, what's wrong?" Fear gripped Red as he recognized some of the same symptoms of the ailment that had taken Cynthia Ann and little Prairie Flower. Others were gathering around Quanah now.

Quanah spoke slowly and with much difficulty; the lame dog, death, was sitting on his chest even now, making his breath short and ragged. "Uncle Red. Carry me outside the fort. Lay me under the big tree. Let the winds blow away this bad spirit."

John Parker, gruff and kind, could hardly hold back a few tears. "Sure, boy, we will. What else can we do? There's a doctor at Waco. Red can ride there. Though he'll be two days in coming back."

"No, no white man doctor. Comanche—*wakan*. Comanche—*wakan*."

"Okay, we'll see what we can do. Red, saddle up that mare. Pearl, get him some grub to take with him. He's going to need his strength for this ride."

Red rode all day on his big roan horse, Beauty, who never seemed to tire. He headed for the rocky ford on the Brazos where he knew Mowray and his peaceful Penatekas might be camped and trading with the even more peaceful Caddos who dwelt around Tehuacana Hill.

It was dusk when he rode into the Indian camp. As he leaped off his horse, he recognized the old Caddo chief who traded horses with the Parkers. He motioned quickly in sign language. "Old Fox, Comanche here, or Comanche gone?"

"Comanche gone."

"Need *wakan*, medicine man. Quanah, our Comanche boy, bad sick."

"Comanche *wakan* gone. Mexican *wakan* here with Caddos." Here he broke out of sign language. "We call her after her Mexican name. *Curandero*. She good. She cure your Quanah."

"Give her your best horse. Tell her to bring all her herbs and medicines. We'll leave as soon as we can see to ride in the morning."

Red slept fitfully, imagining Quanah sleeping on the cold ground, wracked with fever. He had seen the quiet beauty of the Mexican *curandero*. There was a great peacefulness in her eyes. She might have some powerful *wakan* medicine. Red had heard a little bit about the power of some of the desert herbs.

In the morning, Red helped the Mexican woman tie the bundle of herbs tightly to her horse; they mounted and rode away swiftly. The *curandero* on her little gray mare had no trouble keeping up with Red. She plunged through the thickets right behind him, oblivious to scratches from the limbs.

It was early evening when they reached the fort. Nearly everyone was gathered by Quanah as he lay on his pallet under the spreading post oak tree.

The *curandero* quietly took charge. She snapped to a young

Mexican girl servant in Spanish to bring some hot water. To Red, she spoke briefly in English. "Tell all your people to leave us. Go inside. Leave us alone."

Red reluctantly ordered everyone else away. He and John stood at a discreet distance, keeping an eye on the *curandero*'s ministrations to Quanah. When the girl had brought the hot water, she, too, was shooed away.

The *curandero* bathed Quanah's chest and upper limbs in the warm water. She spoke to him in low and reassuring tones. "My name is Dona Teresa. I come from way south, below the Rio Grande. I have been here to learn from the Comanche medicine and from the Caddo medicine. They teach me many of their herbs."

She then took some of the leaves of the prickly ash tree, often called "tickle tongue," and made a poultice in a cloth, soaked it in the hot water, and plastered it to Quanah's chest. Quanah could feel the powerful medicine go forth with the hot water into the pores of his skin. He could feel the tight muscles of his chest relax, soothed by the anodyne of the prickly ash. Now, he could breathe better.

The *curandero* was pleased. She looked at Quanah with compassion. "You respond well, young Quanah. Your spirit is hungry for its medicine. Truly, you are a splendid and handsome man. We must save you. We must teach you about Father Peyote."

At the word peyote, Quanah's ears pricked up. He had heard mention of this strong medicine, but had never seen it. It looked so curious, this brown dried button of a cactus with no thorns. It might have been a piece of leather. The *curandero* handled it very gently as if it were still alive in the ground.

"Father Peyote is very strong. Father Peyote will make you see dreams even when you wake. He will take you into the Spirit Land. There, they will tell you if they want your spirit. If you are to live, they will send your spirit back to your body.

"Do not be afraid. Father Peyote is kind. Here, take a little bit. Chew Father Peyote in your mouth. Swallow the juice that comes to your mouth. Do not swallow Father Peyote. Save Father Peyote for when you need him again."

Quanah looked up into the deep brown eyes that shone above him. He could tell Father Peyote was strong medicine. There was a ringing in his ears. Then his head felt cool and light, as if his scalp were missing. The *curandero*'s face moved away, and Quanah saw only stars. The stars were near and large. They began to move, then burst into color. The red, blue, green, and yellow stars were exploding in the sky.

Suddenly, the stars shifted into a rainbow cloud, with a strong light pulsing behind and through it. As the cloud parted, Quanah saw the face of Noconah, his father, who had eluded his dreams for so long. He knew now he was in the spirit world with his father. He heard two stones hitting each other, and saw his father was teaching him again how to make an arrowhead from the flint. But he knew this! Had he forgotten it? Had he forgotten his people? He chewed Father Peyote more slowly.

Now Noconah's face was drifting away in the rainbow clouds. He was saying something . . . "Go back, Quanah. Go back to the People. Return to the *Nu-mer-nah!*" This name, the only one by which the Comanches called themselves, meant the Real People.

Quanah's eyes were closing now in sleep. The *curandero* was pleased. She knew when Father Peyote brought sleep it was good. She reached in Quanah's mouth and removed the peyote button. Then she applied fresh poultices as long as the water was warm. Finally, she covered Quanah with blankets and lay down beside him to warm his body with hers.

Red and John, watching from a distance, were mystified, but they felt she knew what she was doing. They turned and went into the fort to get some sleep themselves.

When morning came, Quanah awoke to find the *curandero* asleep in the crook of his arm, her warm breasts pressed into his ribs. He knew she had healed him. His mind was clear and he felt his body regaining strength.

"Dona Teresa. Dona Teresa."

"Yes, young Quanah?" She sat up, smiling, putting some distance between them, though pleased with their intimacy.

"Please tell me about Father Peyote. Tell me how to find him, how to use him."

"Your mind is bright, young Quanah. Father Peyote has healed you. Father Peyote is not hard to find. He dwells in the Chisos Mountains in the great bend of the Rio Grande, the home of the Mescalero Apache. The Comanche who fears not the Apache can find Father Peyote easily. After you find Father Peyote, keep him for many moons, almost a year, before you talk to him with your tongue. Then Father Peyote will be kind, though Father Peyote can still be angry and make you suffer. Even when Father Peyote makes you suffer, it is good."

Quanah shrugged off the blankets and rose shakily to his feet. "Father Peyote makes me suffer a little bit now.' He walked to the edge of the clearing and vomited on the bushes. Now his stomach felt good, clear like his head.

"Come, Dona Teresa. I help you carry these blankets." Dona Teresa was quite surprised, for it was unlike a Comanche to do any chore that women could do. She saw the greatness of Quanah's spirit in the warm smile in his eyes.

The Parkers were greatly relieved Quanah was getting well. Though none felt close to him, they treasured his presence, his quiet ways in their midst. They appreciated the catfish and occasional deer he brought to their table. It was with deep regret they woke one morning to find he had left them.

Five nights after the *curandero* had cured him, Quanah gathered his arrows, his one good steel knife, and the hidescraper that had been his mother's. He slipped his gray speckled pony out of the fort and rode away under the half moon toward the Comanches. Quanah was returning home to his people.

CHAPTER XII   CLEAR FORK OF THE BRAZOS

Mackenzie relished these orders; he was to move the Comanche reservation on the Clear Fork of the Brazos to Fort Sill. All the Comanches were being pushed north of the Red River.

The peaceful Penatekas had been settled here on the Clear Fork of the Brazos for some time now. After the manner of the Pueblos, they grew corn, beans, and other vegetables, and depended on hunting to supplement their diet; buffalo and antelope meat were not staples with them as with the Quohadi and Cotʼn-cho-tekas of the high plains.

Mowray had led his people in peace for a long time. Ever since the courthouse fight in San Antonio, Mowray knew the white man would stop at nothing to get his way, and was capable of much treachery.

Rather than taking the vengeance road, Mowray had accommodated, as best he could, the demands of the white man. When the government gave him and his people the reservation on the Clear Fork, he took it. He had learned much in peaceful trade with the pyramid builders to the east; as a young boy he had been on a raid deep in old Mexico, and had seen one of the great pyramids built there. He knew there was greatness in a people who stayed in one place, as well as in those like the plains Comanche, who rode with the wind.

He knew this land on the Brazos was good for raising corn, that the sweet pecans came every other fall, and that the juicy pears from the prickly cactus were easily gathered each summer.

With the fish in the river, there was no reason his people should ever go hungry. Many Comanches did not eat fish, as they believed it turned to poison in the stomach, but the Caddos had taught Mowray's tribe how to smoke and salt the fish so it would keep.

Mowray had come to like the tall, bearded government agent, Robert Neighbors, who had to live with them. He told them about what the Great White Father in Washington thought. Neighbors lived in a one-room log cabin near the falls, but ate as simply as the Comanches. Most important, he was a buffer between them and the white settlers to the east at Jacksboro and Weatherford. Neighbors made peace as best he could between the two races. The peace was hard to keep sometimes. Mowray knew that some of his people were often at fault, as well as the more belligerent white people.

There was the time when an unknown band of Comanches caught a farmer outside of Weatherford in his field of ripe pumpkins. Perhaps he said something that angered them, or perhaps it was the strange vegetable from the east that triggered their ire, but nonetheless they killed the white farmer by spread-eagling him on the ground and bombarding his head with pumpkins.

In Jacksboro, a rabid Indian-hater published a newspaper called *White Man!* The white man had to remind himself of the fact that he *was* white in a land that had been the red man's since time immemorial. Many a hunter and trapper would take the Comanche to wife—for their women were very womanly—and their offspring would be raised more red than white.

Mowray knew all this, and thus was thankful that a man as wise, good, and thoughtful as Neighbors was the government agent, one who could ameliorate conflicts between the two peoples. Once he had asked Neighbors what his name meant, and Neighbors had replied, "Friendly." Mowray thought it was good. The Caddo, the remnants of the old mound-builders, said their name meant "friendly," too.

Now the hawk-faced bluecoat was in their camp. He was riding his big brown stallion up and down. Neighbors was at his side, astride a gray Indian pony, shouting and yelling at Mackenzie. Mowray, with his deep curiosity about human nature, wished he could hear what they said. . . .

"Goddammit, Mackenzie! Your orders be damned! You can't ride in here like this and herd all these people up to Indian Territory like cattle."

"You read the orders." A faint smile played at the corners of Mackenzie's mouth. "Besides, these Comanches are used to moving!"

"Not these. Not Mowray and his tribe! Their corn is just now up and starting to grow and ripen. Move them now and you rob them of six months of work."

"They'll be fed at Fort Sill. There's standard government rations for all the hostiles there."

"Yeah! Jail rations! This is food these people have made themselves. And they're not hostile. They're settled Indians. Can't you see that? Are you blind?"

"You'll see how blind I am. Calhoun, go tell Mowray he's got 'til daybreak to be ready to move. Tell him we'll be posted completely around his camp and will shoot anyone who tries to escape. And you, Neighbors, will you stay here, or come along with us?"

"I'm coming with you, you fool!" He wheeled his horse to ride after Calhoun and somehow try to explain to Mowray this betrayal, this reversal of the white man's word.

The Comanches left more than than they took; they simply had not enough horses and travois. As it was, they toiled through the night, and started on the forced march utterly exhausted.

The bluecoats were all on horseback; their pressure set the pace of the march. Mowray walked behind to gather up his tribe, the old men and women, and some of the young ones, as they fell.

After Neighbors had told Mowray what they must do, Mowray had said it would be done. Now he spoke nothing to Neighbors, and heard nothing from him. Neighbors must learn to endure in silence as did the Comanche.

Mowray buried many of his tribe on the trail to Fort Sill. More importantly, he buried his dream of living alongside the white man as friend and neighbor.

Mackenzie was exultant when they arrived at the fort. He exclaimed to Sherman and Miles, "Now, we've got the Comanches north of a line, the Red River. When they head south, they'll be fair game, and my men will get them."

Sherman had a sharp rebuke for him. "You may know that. There are still five thousand Comanches on the plains who don't know, and don't care, that the Red River is the boundary of their land. Before you get too rambunctious, wait until we gather all the chiefs in the spring for our Medicine Lodge treaties. If, after that, Texas is still subject to raids, then you can start your rabbit drives."

Mackenzie didn't think much of Sherman, and was aware that Sherman probably knew it. Sherman had been a banker before the war, and like many bankers, had a tight little lock on his mind. Nonetheless, he was as fierce as a plucked Bantam rooster, so Mackenzie buttoned his lip, screwed down his hat, gathered his men, and rode back to Fort Concho.

Neighbors had made one last effort to speak to the recalcitrant Mowray. He had told him he would go to Washington and plead their case with the President, and that he would get them back their land on the Clear Fork.

Mowray knew it was useless, and dismissed Neighbors with a gentle wave of his hand. Mowray would sit here on the red clay prairie of Oklahoma and wait for death to come to him and his people. He knew in his bones that the white men, who could herd his people hundreds of miles like cattle, could also one day slay them like cattle.

Perhaps Neighbors, too, felt defeat. Instead of going to Washington, he returned south to Jacksboro. There, only a few short weeks after trailing with the Comanches up to Oklahoma, he was gunned down from behind by an unknown assailant. The law, such as it was, did little or nothing to apprehend whoever had slain this man Neighbors, who befriended the Comanches and championed their cause.

CHAPTER XIII — COMANCHE PEAK

Quanah rode for four days and nights before he reached the mountain. A dried antelope hide on his back, an Appaloosa pony the color of pecan smoke between his legs, he passed over the land like a phantom; only the most watchful would have caught sight of him. He had gauged his journey to arrive at the mountain before daybreak. He wanted to avoid the eyes of the white settlers, whose rock chimneys were scattered ever more frequently along this reach of the Brazos river.

He dismounted and led his horse slowly among the cedar brakes that thronged the rim of the peak. It was actually a plateau, not a peak, a remnant of the dim past when the caprock reached this far south. Now it was like a great ship of rock sailing, inch-by-year, down the great river.

The whites called it Comanche Peak. Few went up on it, though they loved to hunt in the timbers that bordered it. *Ate-nah-wah-che* was one name Quanah's people had given it, which means "sharp smell of cedar," or more precisely "let cedar strike my nose." For nearly two centuries the Comanches had made their bows from the heavy cedar on these slopes, bows that would bend but not break. The huge old grandfather trees near the summit, however, showed no cuts; their great age was their protection. Quanah tied his horse in one of the thickest groves and continued on foot, skirting the top of the plateau, treading past the limestone caves where he had played as a boy.

At the easternmost lip of the mountain, he cautiously climbed up on the table top. Luck. He was alone. In the morning light the river peeked through the willows and cottonwoods here and there like streaks of silver. Quanah slowly straightened up; stretched to his full height, he stood four to eight inches taller than most Comanches or Kiowas. He walked to the side of a great cedar tree where someone looking up from the distance of the valley floor would confuse his body with the trunk of the tree. Immobile, he stood and waited for the sun to dawn. In the gray nether-light paling into day, the land for fifty miles filled his eyes. Below rolled the river where he had first gone swimming. Down the slopes that folded into a draw he had killed his first deer at the age of ten. That memory was still fresh in his mind: the hour he spent stalking the deer with the arrow notched in the bow, the aim that drove the stone through the heart of the fleet animal. Though he had killed many deer since, the memory of how his body trembled to let fly that arrow ten years before was oldest and strongest.

Now the sun arose. A ball of fire still touching the basket of the earth, the sun called to Quanah. He stretched forth his arms and prayed to the Great Spirit: *"Ha-he-ah, Ha-he-e-aaah. . . . Ha-he-ah, ha-he-e-aaahhh."* Only the chant filled his heart as the fierce Texas sun filled the bowl of the sky with its fire.

Wary still, like a wild deer, he dropped to the path that girdled the rim of the peak. He circled back to the shallow limestone cave, stopping only to gather some fresh cedar leaves, cedar bark, and a stubby round cactus, kin to peyote, from the earth. The floor of the rock cave was covered with dry cedar leaves; he sat down cross-legged, laid the cactus and cedar bark beside his feet, then sat and meditated.

Many thoughts from the past flashed through his mind. There was the first war party he had followed, behind Horse Back who adopted him when Noconah was killed and Naduah was captured. Horses were the object of the raid, but they killed the white eyes, too—settlers and a small posse, not knowing their strength, had followed them. They captured one young boy on that raid, and Quanah took special pains to teach him the way of the Comanche. He taught him how to catch rabbits and shoot squirrels with his bow, so the young men, instead of scoffing, would admire his prowess at hunting. He taught him how to rub red clay into his skin so the young girls would not laugh at his paleness. Quanah named the young boy Tejas. When the brothers of his mother came and took him from Horse Back's tent, he had to forget his young friend, Tejas. When he returned to the Comanches, he learned Tejas had been killed in a raid.

Quanah thought of the time when he and his father and mother pulled up stakes in the dead of night and moved off this flat mountain, where he now sat, to the fork of the Brazos where the water ran sweet. His father did not speak to him, but rode back and forth in the camp shouting urgently to the tribe. His mother spoke only one word, "Soldiers." Never since had he visited this peak. He spotted it many other times, and the effect of seeing it, but not setting foot on its slopes, served to enlarge it in his memory. Now he was here, sitting on the smooth limestone, smelling the pungent cedars. Along with the deep peace that filled him stirred a grain of bitterness towards that which had kept him for so long from coming here.

His thoughts turned to the settlers, the farmers, and the cattlemen who were crowding west from Fort Worth and Dallas. Across the river lived the sons of the great white warrior, Crockett, who had slain such great numbers of the Mexicans in San Antonio. Up the river was the small settlement of Granbury, named by the Texanos for their chief who was killed in the war they fought with their brothers east of the Great River. Above the town were the older settlers, those who had stood their ground against Quanah's people. He knew their names as well as his own; they were Peveler, Porter, Thorp, Kinnon, Marrs, and Blevins. He respected them as worthy enemies; they built their houses of thick stone, and their eyes were sharp like hawks' eyes. He never caught one of them alone.

The weight of memory pulled him further back he let the thoughts of his boyhood come and go of their own accord. One lingered—the time when his father first took him to the little bald mountain, where the Kinnons now settled, and taught him how to shape the flint. He had played at making crude arrowheads with other boys, and fastened the rough pieces of stone to rough shafts and shot at birds. But this was different. His father taught him how to make the long, sharp-pointed head for deer and buffalo, and the flat, broad arrowhead for war. He showed Quanah the quickest ways to chip the flint—for, if an enemy approached, there was no need for perfection—and the slow, painstaking way that yielded flints crafted so precisely that he could retrieve them time and again from his quarry.

He was back there with his father on that bald hill that sat on the river, called Tompson Mountain for the Tompson family who first settled on the chipping grounds, and for their trouble were slain by the Comanches. He was hefting the large flint and chipping at the smaller flat rock until he had the rough triangular shape of the head. Carefully and slowly, he would heat the arrowhead stuck in the fork of a stick and drip water along its edge, chipping off tiny round flakes of flint until it was sharp. When he was finished, his father, whose deep-red face was broad and flat in contrast to Quanah's finely chiseled features, would run his thumb along the edge of the stone and grunt his approval, then smile.

He remembered gathering firewood and buffalo chips for his mother's cookfire, and asking her about the white people. She told him that the way of the Comanche was best. The whites were greedy, and could not abide by agreements to leave the land of the Quohadi alone. She told him, sometimes slapping herself smartly on the cheek to drive the point home, that the Comanche would have to fight for a long time before their lands were secure, and that Quanah must grow to be a great warrior for his people.

Then a deep sadness seeped into him and began to cramp his chest as he thought of the death of his father and the capture of his mother and little sister by the Texanos. That was when Horse Back took Quanah into his tent and treated him as his own son.

Quanah remembered his days living with the white Parkers, now like a dream. The ways of the Parkers were strange. Quanah never came to like their food and their clothes. After only a few short months with them, he fell ill with the same sickness that had taken his mother. Then his Uncle Red found the Mexican *curandero* who came and healed him and taught him of Father Peyote. When he chewed on the peyote, he knew it was far stronger than chewing tobacco. His spirit swirled like a far-spreading oak in a great wind. He saw as through a cloud the face of his father. When he asked his father if he would die, Noconah had said, "No, you will not die, my son."

Myriad images divided into bright colors, like the sun split by a blade of grass, and fluttered through his mind until his eyes were tired from trying to catch them. He slept, and the *curandero* knew the spell was deep. During the last threshold of sleep, Quanah knew he would not die, and that the spirit of sickness would depart before the power of the peyote.

Before the *curandero* left, she pressed into Quanah's hand a small leather pouch containing a button of the dream herb. *"Padre Peyotl, el grande sueno,"* she spoke to Quanah. "Carry it with you and it will protect you. Eat it only when you stand in need of great medicine."

This flood of memories washed through Quanah's mind as he sat on the lip of the mountain. Soon, he was completely still, unmoving as the rocks. A female redbird flitted down from a cedar to light on his knee, a cedarberry in her beak. He noted her presence, much as one might look casually down the corner of an eye and see one's own nose. The redbird dropped the cedarberry between Quanah's folded legs and flew away into the cedar brakes, her brown and red wings beating a soft whir in his ear.

All day he sat and took neither food nor water. On his journey he drank only from the leather water sack slung from his neck, and ate nothing. As the sun sank in the western sky, Quanah turned his head to let the rays strike him full in the face where he sat under the low-slung ledge of limestone. Another hour passed, then two, then three. He must be sure the Texanos in the valley were asleep and would not see his fire.

When he was ready, he gathered together dried cedar leaves and the cedar bark and twigs from the smooth stone floor of the open-mouthed cave. He struck flint to flint and made his fire. Between himself and the flames he laid a piece of napped buffalo hide. On this he placed his pipe, his fan of eagle feathers, and the leather pouch holding Father Peyote that the *curandero* had pressed into his hand not so many moons ago. The night was quiet save for a few whippoorwills tossing their mournful song back and forth on the slopes of the mountain. Now and then he heard the foxes bark, and he knew none would disturb him. The smell of the crushed, fresh cedar leaves mingled with the smell of the cedar smoke curling along the limestone roof bit sharply at his nose. He placed some of the leaves on the fire to increase the smoke.

He felt for the tobacco in his hunting pouch. Finding it, he rolled a quid in thin strips of cedar bark, placed it in his pipe, and lit it with a glowing stick from the fire. With deep puffs from his pipe, he added to the smoke from the fire, and smiled. The medicine would be strong, as thick as this smoke. A song from the ancients welled within him; having no drum, his palm slapped the rhythm on his knee as the chant rolled up from his chest to his tongue. He smoked and sang until the tobacco was gone. His eyes, full of smoke, no longer stung.

He loosed the neck of the pouch and peeled it back until the button of Father Peyote stood vivid in the firelight. His heart brimming with thanks to the Great Spirit, he lifted the button to his mouth. He chewed it slowly, savoring each bitter drop of juice the peyote brought. He chewed and he waited.

    First, there came a roaring in his ears, like the sound of the running hooves of many buffalo, heard from afar. His eyes turned inward, searched each corner of his mind, then turned to the sky which opened like a door across the roof of his skullcap.
    Father Peyote still chewed in his mouth.
    The first dim shape danced in and out of the clearing. The blur faded. Coyote? No. The shape grew large and dark. Wolf. Wolf, who grew tall in the mountains. Wolf, who loped the long prairies outpacing the buffalo. Wolf, whose night song to the Great Spirit hushed all other songs. Wolf, whose nose was long, whose ears were long and sharp and keen as knives. Wolf, who taught his younger brother, man, with naught but a look from his eyes. As quickly as he had come, Wolf . . . gone.
    Now Quanah saw a pole in the clearing. The blue faded. Now the red and yellow colors were warm and dancing.

Absently, his right hand plucked the fan of eagle feathers and moved slowly through the air bringing the cedar smoke to and from his face with heavy sweeps.

    The pole grew long and slim. A spear. The spear of his father, Noconah, painted red, which stood in the tent of Horse Back, its long flint blade stuck in the ground. Quanah stretched out his left hand to grasp the spear. On the limestone walls of the cave, flickering in the firelight, was the shadow of a Comanche warrior gripping the air with his hand. . . .
    His hand touched the spear . . . the spear changed shape. Spear shook in his hand, turned into a snake. The snake grew into his arm as he drew it, wriggling backward, through the air: the sign of the Comanche. The eagle feathers stirred. Now into the clearing flew his namesake, Eagle—the eagle with the bald head. Eagle he was. Eagle he knew. . . . Quanah. . . . Eagle. . . . Serpent Eagle of the Comanche.
    The eagle clutched the snake in its claws. The snake twisted and shook, but could not squirm free. The circle closed. The air

filled with the beating of the hovering eagle's wings. Quanah was held by the eagle and bent back toward the earth. As he passed into the spirit world, he felt the brush of the eagle's wings on his face. The clearing faded. . . . his eyes closed.

He woke while it was still dark, the medicine strong upon him, as if he had not slept. He drank a long draught of water. Then he took his sharply honed flint knife and sliced into the cactus, little brother to Father Peyote taken from the holy mountain. Peeling the bristles back, he cut and ate the fresh pulp, cleansing his mouth. His vision returned. He would remember this night many times. He would remember all that had been done.

Quanah turned his eyes to the sky. Two more hours of darkness. There was time enough to ride to the chalk mountain just to the west and raid Barnard's trading post for a fresh supply of tobacco. Barnard would be asleep and would not see Quanah. Even should he wake, it would be but to sleep again.

Quanah gathered Father Peyote, fan, and pipe carefully, scattered the ashes of his fire with his hand, and rescattered the dry leaves across the limestone porch. In the cedar thicket, his hungry horse nuzzled his side as he untied the rope halter. Quanah knew the first thing he would do when he rode into the camp of the Quohadi. He would retrieve the spear of his father from the tent of Horse Back and ride among the camps with it held high above his head. Many braves would follow him now. No longer was there a smell of the white man to his name. As he rode his pony in the predawn dark toward the shadow of the chalk mountain, he carried the look and bearing of the eagle.

CHAPTER XIV   BOSQUE RIVER

The small band of Comanches rode south to the double mountain fork of the Brazos, crossed it, and swung wide around the double wings of the big two-headed mountain. The great heap of limestone, one shelf rearing towards the east, one towards the west, made Quanah think of his eagle once more. Here was a great stone eagle flying up from, then alighting, upon the earth. Now they were at the clear fork, near Mowray's camp. Where was Mowray?

The Comanche warriors started shouting loud whoops of astonishment and wrath as they rode around and poked through the remnants of Mowray's camp. They saw many valuables—clothes, tools, weapons—they knew no one would leave behind. The puzzlement turned into a molten wrath. Quanah spotted a red clay bank on a creek running into the Clear Fork from the south. He let out a yell.

The eight young warriors followed him to the mud bank where they leapt from their horses, and splashing their hands in the water, scooped up the red clay, slicking and smearing it on their arms, chest, and face.

On his chest, Quanah painted a sun in yellow clay with red rays streaming from it, remembering the time he saw the eagle on the medicine mounds come wheeling out of the sun, the light chasing it.

Now to their ponies. Man and horse blended as they sped south, the taste for blood and revenge for whatever had happened at Mowray's camp bitter on their tongues. The prairie was broken only by ravines where the draws sucked the spring water from the limestone buttes to the west.

As evening fell and the sun dipped its feathers in the western plains, Quanah led his war party down into the shadows of the river the Mexicans called Bosque, for its thick woods.

By swinging a wide loop to the west, the Comanches had dropped below the line of settlements where fear of an Indian raid bred alertness. Here was a ranch with a corral full of fine horses. The stoutly built log house was already closed for the night, though a yellow glow through the windows meant someone was still awake.

Quanah directed his men carefully. Two braves would slip up on foot to open the corral. Five more would ride into the corral and drive the horses out, while the last would ride down with horses for the two braves on foot.

Quanah rode his horse very quietly to the corner of the log house on the side opposite the corral. He would meet the enemy first.

All went as Quanah hoped. The poles were slipped from the corral gates, and his men rode down. As the horses were pouring through the gate however, one or two whinnied their surprise. Quanah was ready. The front door of the house opened violently, and the rancher, a big strapping man with handlebar moustaches and wearing longjohns, swung his Winchester to his shoulder. He turned as he heard Quanah's horse surge towards him.

Even knowing that the man would kill him if he could, the coup was enough for Quanah. He swung the flint axe down flat on the back of the man's head, and snatched the rifle out of his hands as he crumpled in the dust. Ishtai, Otter Belt, and Gray Wolf joined him as they chased after the others and the large band of horses they had captured.

They drove the horses for hours that night, for the air was cool and the moon full. Toward daybreak they stopped where a small stream splashed over a limestone ledge on a branch of the Paluxy, watered their horses, walked off the bloat, then watered them again. Quanah knew he had put a few hours between his band and wouldbe pursuers. But he knew, too, that they would be followed. He knew the easy path up onto the caprock, which with so many horses would help them. But Quanah suspected the ranchers also knew that easy slope and, by riding straight for it, might catch him there. So, he swung farther north where the Salt Fork of the Brazos came off the caprock. The climb would be harder, and the water bad, but his horses, his bounty, would be secure.

When they finally rode into Horse Back's camp in the heart of the Palo Duro Canyon, there was great rejoicing. The horses were many. They added to the wealth of the whole tribe. Moreover, a new leader was born, this tall, lean Quanah, whom some called Skunk and others called Eagle.

CHAPTER XV   PALO DURO CANYON

Tonarcy was the oldest and loveliest daughter of Ten Bears. One could say Quanah had had his eyes on her as had every other young man in the tribe, and not a few of the older ones. Tonarcy, though, opened her eyes and batted her lashes only for Quanah. It was fitting and proper, now that Quanah had horses, he should come calling on the formidable Ten Bears, and persuade him to let Tonarcy spread her skirt in Quanah's tent.

Few in the tribe were unaware of what was taking place. Ten Bears was in his tent, waiting for Quanah, his new son-in-law, to make his offer. Tonarcy had already gathered her belongings into a buffalo robe on the advice of Kenanah, the wife of Horse Back, who knew about such things.

When Quanah spoke a loud greeting before the flap of the tepee, Ten Bears said, "Come in, my son. The turtle was here some time ago, and said you would be along. Come and sit by my knee and drink this mesquite tea my wife made. It is thick and strong and bitter. It will do you good."

"Ten Bears, old father and warrior. My heart is so full my tongue lodges in my throat. You know how the sun stirs up the fire in a young man's loins towards certain young women."

"Yes, I know. I remember how it was with me. You know, young

51

Quanah, Tonarcy is very dear to her old father."

"Yes, I know. Even the prairie grass likes to hold the dew away from the sun. I ask only for what is right, old great battler."

"Yes, Quanah. My spirit tells me you are right for Tonarcy. Your strength will be a match for her beauty. Tell me, what have you brought to replace the empty spot in Ten Bears' heart when Tonarcy is gone."

"Ten Bears has good ears. Can he not hear the hooves pawing the ground?"

"Ah! Quanah has brought me a horse he stole from the Texanos!"

"No, not one horse."

"Then Quanah brings me two horses, one for me, and one for my travois."

"No, Quanah does not bring two horses."

"Then you bring me three new, big, strong horses; one for me, one for my travois, and one for my wife who doesn't like to walk either."

"No, not three horses."

Ten Bears exclaimed, "You bring four!" for four would be a high price to pay for any daughter.

Quanah smiled a little, happy that his gift of horses exceeded Ten Bears' expectations.

"No, not four."

"Come then, let us go outside and see what you bring old Ten Bears to hold him up in his old age."

Outside, Ten Bears grunted in admiration over the five big horses Quanah brought him. They were red and sorrel mares, and Ten Bears knew that crossing them with Appaloosas would produce the beautiful red and white paint colts that the Comanches prized so much. "Ah, my son, Tonarcy is a good bargain for you. She will bear you many sons and keep your feet warm many a cold winter."

Quanah was supremely happy now, though a bit shy and diffident as he placed Tonarcy astride her pony with her belongings and led her off to her new home in his tepee. Tonarcy was hard pressed to hide her smiles and giggles as the other young maidens in the camp laughed and wondered at her fate.

That night, after Tonarcy prepared Quanah a meal and the camp was quiet, they disrobed and lay together naked upon a buffalo robe, bathed in the golden light of the dying campfire.

Tonarcy was more desirable in nearly every way than most women, and for Quanah, more than all women; he ran his hands over her full breasts and the curves of her beautifully rounded hips and thighs. The heat was strong in him now. Tonarcy accepted him with shining eyes.

Their love beat with the thunder and the quickness of the Comanche waterdrum. Tonarcy, aroused by the passion of her Quanah, arched her back to meet him. For both, the end of the love-making was a little bit like dying, or the lassitude of slowly waking from a beautiful dream. Neither wanted it to end.

CHAPTER XVI   FORT CONCHO

    Mackenzie often wondered why the hell he came to Texas. He was mindful of Sherman saying that "if he owned both hell and Texas, he would live in hell, and rent out Texas." When the wind blew off the western plains, the skin constantly chafed red under the stinging dust. The Comanches were still raiding into Texas. They still thought it was their domain. When he rode out after the Comanches, they sank into the limitless expanse of prairie, or perhaps into the ground. Perhaps they were only ghosts whose spirits walked abroad at night. Perhaps there were no Comanches.

    His Tonkawa scouts assured him the Comanches were still out there. Of course they were paid to track Comanches, so they must have some to track. If only they didn't quit when they got their wages and go off on their splendid drunks to Waco.

    He listened more to Calhoun. Calhoun knew the Comanches and he knew Texas. Though there wasn't a tooth in his head, Calhoun had held onto his scalp through a half dozen Comanche raids.

    "Calhoun! Come here a minute."

    "Yes, sir!"

    "And bring that coffee pot with you when you come."

    "Yes, sir."

    "There, that's better. This is damn good coffee, Calhoun, considering it's made with river water."

"The secret is not to let the water get too hot. The Conchos River is a bit muddy, but it's a sweet water river compared to the Brazos."

"What's the Brazos like?"

"Well, the Salt Fork runs off those alkali flats and makes it mighty salty. Myself, I could never get used to it. Some people take a liking to it. They say the trailhands with Chisholm on his traildrives packed salt on up into Oklahoma and Kansas to put in their coffee so it would taste like coffee made with Brazos River water."

Mackenzie smiled and burst out laughing when he realized how near he had come to believing Calhoun's tall tale. Calhoun smiled.

"Tell me, Calhoun, how the Brazos came to get its name."

"Well, Colonel, it shows on the maps, the Spanish maps, all the way back to Coronado. I reckon when they gave up looking for the Gran Quivira and headed east off those dry plains of the Llano Estacado, they were getting to be mighty thirsty.

"I don't reckon the Pueblos would have told them where all the waterholes were. After you leave the Pecos east of Santa Fe, there ain't nothing until you ride off the caprock. I've always pictured that Spanish scout spotting shallow water in a flat muddy draw on the headwaters of the Brazos, running and jumping face first into it with arms spread out, then splashing that water up into his bushy beard and dust-caked ears and muttering 'Ah! The Arms of God!' 'Cause that's what the whole Spanish name means: the Brazos de Dios, the Arms of God. The Comanche name for it means the water of the deep blue sky. That's because of the sandstone formations where the salty water clears up in summer and becomes as blue as the roasted heavens overhead."

"Calhoun, you rode with Robert E. Lee here in Texas back during the fifties, didn't you?"

Calhoun lowered his eyes and shifted about nervously. "Yes, sir, I did do that."

"What was he like, this Lee, when you rode with him?"

"Well, sir, he was a good soldier, kind to his men and his horses. None sat a horse better. We must have rode sixteen hundred miles together when we bivouaced up the Brazos and back down the Colorado."

"Tell me, Calhoun, was Lee kind to the Comanches?"

Calhoun knew the answer Mackenzie wanted, but that was not the answer he gave. "Yes, sir. Master Lee thought the Comanche to be a better Injun. One capable of Christian charity. And he said he never saw better horsemen than the Comanches."

Mackenzie's smile twisted away into a sort of resentment. "Well, that's nice to know. So Lee had Christian charity for the Comanche. I wish he had shown a bit more of that Christian charity toward us at Cold Harbor and at Petersburg, when the game was already up for him."

"Beg pardon, sir, but for Master Lee, it weren't no game."

"Damn, Calhoun. Damn you and your Lee. We've got to fight these Comanches or they'll get us! You hear me! They'll get us! Turn in. We hit patrol at first light!"

CHAPTER XVII CONCHOS RIVER

Quanah saw another horse raid as the quickest way to increase his wealth. To the Comanches, the horse determined the way of life. They constantly moved their camp to be nearer the vast herds of buffalo migrating north and south over the great plains. The warrior with many horses never went without meat. The warrior with many horses never went without a wife to cook the meat or to carry his offspring.

Tonarcy was more wife than Quanah could have wished for; already her belly was swelling with their first child. Tonarcy needed more horses to carry their travois, to make the moving of their camp easier when they moved to the winter home in Palo Duro Canyon.

His stature as a chief was also related to the number of horses he owned. The Comanches only selected one Great Chief, the war chief of all the tribes, and as a balance to him, one great medicine chief. Below these two chiefs, each tribe or clan had its chief, and below each clan chieftain were many lesser chiefs. In short, one was a chief if other braves would ride with him, whether in pursuit of game, bounty, or glory. Chiefs were made by their exploits, though it helped, as with Quanah, if the father had been a chief also.

After Quanah's first successful horse raid, many braves wanted to ride with him. They saw that Quanah had found his medicine and his medicine was strong. On this raid were Ishtai, who knew a strange medicine; Otter Belt, Quanah's closest friend from his boyhood; Red Horse, one of the stoutest and strongest warriors; and Lone Wolf, one of the stealthiest. More had wanted to come, but Quanah desired only a small band that could more quietly slip unseen down the river valleys.

This time, they swung much farther west before heading south, striking some of their old watering holes on the headwaters of the Conchos River. Their foes, the Lipan and Mescalero Apaches, had been pushed south into the mountains of Mexico near the army forts in the Davis Mountains and at the junction of the North and South Conchos.

As the slight canyon began to deepen, Quanah led his band up onto the limestone bluff that overlooked the stream on the west. The cover was less but they could see farther down the river. Lone Wolf topped the rise first, then ducked and swung his pony around and rode back toward Quanah, his heart jumping. He knew now that Quanah intended to steal some of the bluecoats' horses at the fort.

"Quanah, up the canyon, not far, are many bluecoats, all on horseback. We go?"

"No. Red Horse, hold our horses. We will watch the bluecoats for a little while." Quanah, Lone Wolf, Ishtai, and Otter Belt all leaped off and crawled hurriedly up the hill. Red Horse drew the horses deeper into the shadows of a thick grove of post oaks, impenetrable even to a hawk's eye.

From the brow of the ridge, Quanah could see the bluecoats falling out to make camp in the almost dry river bed not a hundred yards below him. They bivouaced quickly and started campfires to warm their coffee and boil some water to soften their hardtack. Quanah spoke under his breath to Ishtai and the others. "I know this leader of the bluecoats. That's Mackenzie, who came when I was with the white Parkers."

"Mackenzie!" Ishtai exclaimed harshly. "Mackenzie was the one who destroyed Mowray's camp and herded his people to the reservation at Fort Sill like cattle. I would like to kill this Mackenzie."

Quanah listened closely to Ishtai and studied him with his liquid brown eyes. "Ishtai, you and I will ride into the bluecoats' camp. We will talk to Mackenzie."

Otter Belt and Lone Wolf were as stunned by these words as Ishtai. For a moment they thought Quanah had surely lost his mind.

As Quanah unfolded his plan, their looks of stunned amazement turned to admiration. Quanah spoke slowly, his hand indicating in gestures how they would make their move.

"I know Mackenzie. He is hard and strong. He is the best chieftain the bluecoats have. Still, he will remember Quanah. When Quanah rides in with a white flag, he will want to talk with Quanah and feed Quanah meat. Quanah knows what Mackenzie would like to know. Mackenzie will want to use Quanah as bait for his trap, but Quanah will be bait for Quanah's trap.

"The bluecoats are tired. When they sleep, only one or two will be awake to watch their horses. Should Mackenzie make captive Ishtai and Quanah, you, Lone Wolf, will come at night and free us, and Red Horse and Otter Belt will get the bluecoats' horses. Should Mackenzie treat us like friends, then all five of us will unhobble the horses, count coup on the watchmen, and the bluecoats will not have a single horse with which to pursue."

The other warriors saw the cunning in Quanah's plan and breathed their ready assent to it. It was a good plan.

At the mott of post oaks, they explained it to Red Horse. Red Horse would bring the Comanche ponies up the draw at the last moment so the Comanches would have their own trained mounts when they stampeded the soldiers' horses.

Mackenzie was talking to Calhoun at the campfire in front of his tent. "So you say your General Lee was fond of the Comanches he encountered on his Texas tour?"

"No, sir, not fond. Rather, he was kind toward them. He knew they were savages, but he reckoned they were men like himself, and saw quickly that many had intelligence; in certain chiefs, there was even sagacity."

"Humph! Little better than animals if you ask me. Would you marry one of their squaws, Calhoun?"

"Well, sir, I can't rightly say. My grandfather did, and I don't think he ever complained about it. I've known friends of mine to marry them, especially the Caddos and Comanches, and they say they can't be beat."

Mackenzie cast a colder glance at this toothless old Texan who was his guide. So, he had Indian blood, too. Where would his loyalties lie, if it came to a fight? This was a strange land, and a strange people. These Texans either hated the Comanches, or loved them, or cohabited with them. In any case, they had no clear idea of controlling them as Mackenzie had. Here was his trusted aide, who slept outside his tent, who had Indian blood in him. . . .

"What, what's this! Two damn Indians riding up here!"

Calhoun spoke sharply. "Hold your rifles down, boys. They come peacefully. Here's two of those 'animals,' Colonel. Looks like they want to talk to you."

Quanah and Ishtai, unperturbed by the rifles leveled at them, rode right up to Mackenzie. Mackenzie did not recognize the full-grown warriors, though there was something familiar about the face of one of them.

Quanah broke the pregnant silence. "Mackenzie. We meet once more. Me, Quanah Parker!"

A relieved smile came over both Mackenzie's and Calhoun's faces. Mackenzie barked at his troops, "At ease, men. It's Quanah Parker. Remember a few years back when we first came to Texas. Hell, he's dressed Comanche now, but he's half white. We know him. It's all right."

Little did Mackenzie know, thought Quanah as he and Ishtai slid from their horses. They clasped right hands with Mackenzie and Calhoun, the way white men did to show they held no weapons.

Mackenzie, still a bit nervous, but glad this Comanche had a smidgin of English and more than a smidgin of white blood, asked, "Quanah, what brings you this far west? How are your uncles at Parker's Fort?"

"Uncles are fine. Quanah come west to look for another uncle, Isaac Parker. He was caught by Comanche same time as my mother. Isaac living way west and south with Mexicans. Ishtai come with Quanah. He no can speak English. He speak good Mexican, help Quanah find Isaac."

"Well, sit and have supper here. Nothing but cornbread and beans, but it's filling."

"Thanks, Mackenzie. You good man. You friend to Quanah and Quanah's people."

"Well, the Parkers are a mighty tough breed, Quanah. I still remember you breaking those horses that day. I respect the Parkers for coming down here to Texas and opening up the frontier, I surely do. Corporal, take these horses and care for them."

Quanah, already feeling his authority and mastery of the situation, brushed the corporal's hand aside. "Quanah take care of horses." He told Ishtai in Comanche to tether the horses to a nearby willow, away from the main body of the camp. He withdrew from his bedroll an otter skin and handed it to Mackenzie as a present. Mackenzie was pleased but managed not to show it. "Calhoun, rustle up some plates and some grub for these Injuns."

"Yes, sir!" Calhoun, who had been speaking kindly of the Comanches before, seemed most wary and and suspicious of Quanah and Ishtai. Especially Ishtai. Ishtai was a fullblood and he seemed more nervous than a fox in a henhouse. Calhoun suspected he had never been this close to a white man before; one of the looks he had seen Ishtai give Mackenzie was a look of murder if he had ever seen one.

Ranald Mackenzie drew up his camp stool nearer the fire where Calhoun, Quanah, and Ishtai were wolfing down their plates of beans and hardtack. He relished these Indians riding into his camp. Not fully knowing their purposes, he felt safe, and sensed that he might learn something from this half-breed, Quanah. Quanah, after all, had been living with his white uncles the last time Mackenzie had seen him. That Quanah was now dressed as a Comanche warrior did not register with Mackenzie; Quanah's face seemed open and friendly and free of guile.

Mackenzie had already eaten, and he pulled from his jacket pocket his longstemmed briar pipe and tobacco, the best Virginia burley. He stuffed the pipe and slowly lit it with a twig from the fire. He saw Quanah's eyes light up at the sight of the tobacco. After drawing a few deep draws on it, he handed it to Quanah. "Care for some of this pipe?"

Quanah grunted, nodded, and reached for the pipe bowl, his fingers brushing Mackenzie's hand as he took it. After a few long puffs on it, he passed it to Ishtai, which startled Mackenzie, who was not sure if he would see his pipe return. Ishtai drew deeply and then passed it to Calhoun. Calhoun hesitated a long moment; he was not sure he wanted to smoke this pipe, since he was afraid he might have to kill one or both of these Comanches. Nonetheless, to allay suspicion of his thoughts, he puffed heartily and passed the pipe to Mackenzie.

The evening sun had already sunk behind the mesas to the west, and the high-strung clouds were holding its last gold-red rays as only flat-country clouds can. Quanah said little as he passed the tobacco pipe back and forth between Mackenzie and Ishtai. He seldom glanced at Calhoun. His main intent was to lull Mackenzie's mind; Calhoun's vigilance could be taken care of later.

Mackenzie was thoroughly enjoying the encounter. Here he had come looking for Indians, and two had ridden right into his camp. With a little luck he would gain the information he needed to know.

"Quanah, where are the big Comanche bands at now?"

"Quanah not know. Most Comanche way north. Ok-la-homa. Some Comanche on high plains Mexicans call Llano Estacado."

"What's the band called on the Llano?"

"Quohadi, they the fiercest Comanche. You be lucky, Mackenzie, if you don't meet up with Quohadi!"

Mackenzie's brows lifted a little at this bit of volunteered wisdom. "Quanah, I'll take care of these Quohadi when I run into them. What do you think of the Tonkawas?" Mackenzie was getting two new Tonkawa scouts soon from Fort Richardson.

Quanah's face darkened as though a cloud had passed over it. "Tonkawa is lower than a snake. Tonkawa eat the flesh of his dogs, eat the flesh of his own people."

Calhoun thought Quanah spoke like a true wild Comanche; he planned on getting no sleep this night. Mackenzie laughed at the suggestion of cannibalism. "You have to admit, Quanah, sometimes in these parts there's not much to eat."

Quanah relaxed and smiled. "If have horses, always find game." Again, like a true Comanche, thought Calhoun.

"Well, it's fortunate we have plenty of horses. You're right. Guess we better turn in and get an early start. We'll talk more, Quanah, over breakfast. Here, you take the last of this tobacco, as a sign of Mackenzie's friendship." As the pouch of tobacco passed from his hand to Quanah's, Mackenzie thought fleetingly, what else will this Indian take from me?

This thought came from his sudden awareness that Quanah had power and subtly used his power over Mackenzie; he wanted the tobacco and pulled it from Mackenzie without hesitating.

"Calhoun, bunk here by my tent."

"Aye, sir!"

"Till morning," Quanah returned quietly, as Mackenzie signed off to him with "Till morning."

After Mackenzie had entered his tent, he pulled off his boots, dug *The Wars of Napoleon* from his gear and stretched out on his cot to read by candlelight. He knew the men gained a certain reassurance from seeing the dim glow within his tent.

Calhoun turned to preparing his bunk in front of Mackenzie's tent. Quanah and Ishtai slowly rose and walked down toward the river where they bedded down next to their horses. Many soldiers in camp that night swore they would not sleep, as did Calhoun, but the fatigue of the long hard day in the saddle caught up with them. As the candle burned low in Mackenzie's tent, then snuffed out, they all slept, save Calhoun and the lone picket watch over the horses.

The full moon went down at last; the night deepened. Thick, scattered clouds added to the darkness. Even starlight was dimmed. Calhoun elevated his head so he could see the sleeping forms of the two Comanches. He moved his eyes constantly to keep the images clear, but they always returned to those shadowy but distinct shapes on the white gravel bar.

He must have dozed. Now he saw one of the shapes turning, lifting, and walking slowly toward him. No need to sound the alarm, not just yet. Where was the other shape? He raised up on his elbows, heard a faint sound behind him like the swish of leather, turned his head and glimpsed the flat of Quanah's flint hatchet as it caught him along the temple. Darkness came mercifully over Calhoun's mind, drowning the pain; he later remembered his lips trying to shape an outcry, but no sound came. Only the whippoorwills called out, and they woke no one.

The Comanches moved along the soldiers' horses on all fours, like small horses themselves. They moved slowly, letting the horses get their smell. Not a single horse neighed or whinnied. When they were unhobbled, Quanah loosed the picket rope. Picking out one of the biggest geldings, he led it up the slope, hugging the deeper shadows of the oak motts. The rest of the horses followed, urged on by the other Comanches on horseback.

Once well up on the prairie, Quanah mounted his own horse, led by Lone Wolf. He spoke quietly. "Coyote God has smiled on us tonight. Even he was silent to let the Quohadi steal the horses of the bluecoats. Come, let us ride!"

The Comanches, forming a loose net with Quanah in front, began the horses at a trot, then broke into a lope, then stretched out into a full run across the open prairie. The horses were like straws in the wind that fed the power of the Quohadi.

CHAPTER XVIII
CONCHOS RIVER WALK

Mackenzie was awakened by the shrill blast of the bugle, sounding alarm. He pulled up his suspenders, grabbed his coat and pistol, and stumbled outside in his stocking feet, feeling the cold ground bite sharply.

Calhoun came around slowly, a lump the size of a goose egg on his head. "Colonel, I'm afraid those Comanches have got our horses."

"What! The two of them! God damn those smiling serpents. God damn the wool they pulled over my eyes!" Mackenzie stormed back into his tent and pulled on his boots. When he returned outside with his pistol strapped to his side, the men were falling into muster.

Calhoun, still looking and feeling like he had been kicked by a mule, had taken a quick count. "Men present and accounted for, sir! Burbridge has a knot like mine on the back of his head. Every last one of the horses is gone."

"All right, men. I'm to blame for this. I met and knew this Comanche when he lived with white men. I did not know he had gone back to the blanket and the buffalo. We'll catch his sorry hide out here one of these days, and then we'll make him pay. It appears we must hike the forty miles back to the fort. Take your weapons, rations, and sleeping blankets. Leave your saddles; we'll send a wagon train back for them. Fall out and make your pack. We leave immediately after breakfast."

Mackenzie knew the torture he faced getting back to the fort. At Chancellorsville he had taken a minié ball; it had cut through his horse's neck and his leg and lodged in the back of his knee. The surgeon told him that it was either leave it in or take the leg off. Mackenzie chose to keep his leg, even if he would never have full use of it. He could not walk more than a hundred yards without the dull, stabbing pain returning.

With the men assembled they set out, grumbling and cursing. Mackenzie led them for a quarter mile, and then they started passing him. Calhoun hung back, whittled a willow walking stick, and handed it to Mackenzie.

Mackenzie was grateful for the extra leg. The pain and exertion were already bringing sweat to his brow. "Calhoun, did you guess they would try a trick like that? Why didn't you tell me something?" His voice alternated between passion and whine.

"No, sir. I had strong suspicions of that there Ishtai. But Quanah? No, sir, I believed him just like you did. That Quanah's something alright. I hadn't seen an Injun disguise his thoughts like that in a long time, if ever."

"Disguise! Humph! That's too kind. Deceit is more like it. That lying bastard!"

"But it wasn't just his thoughts. He was there inside our heads mixing up our thoughts. That's medicine for you, Colonel. That's the kind of medicine the Comanches make up stories about."

"Well, we've got medicine too. These navy Colts and these Remington repeaters. We will have a return visit with that stupid half-breed, and give him a dose of our medicine."

"Half-breed, he is. Stupid, no. He's got the cunning of the Comanche and the white man both. I ain't seen nothing like it. No, sir. I don't want to predict, but Colonel, we ain't gonna see Quanah unless he wants us to see him!"

Bitter thought. That night as they camped, Mackenzie tried to sleep through the pain of his swollen leg. He drifted into a fitful doze and saw nothing but Quanah squatted across the campfire, that faint enigmatic smile flitting across his face.

It was a mid-August day. The sky was clear, the wind still, and the Texas sun boiled and scorched along the earth like a cauldron of fire. The soldiers shed their blue coats. The salt from their perspiration dried and crystallized on their woolen underwear. They slowed to a snail's pace so they wouldn't outstrip their commander. Mackenzie heard some of the curses, not all of which were directed at the Comanches.

Mackenzie himself often contributed to the cursing when a jog of the terrain jolted his leg and the sharp pains shot like hot knives down in his ankles and up into his hip and groin. The knee hurt so relentlessly he was unable to even think about it.

The sun poured without mercy from the sky. The white light and white heat blistered the white men's cheeks. Had they been riding horses, they might have stopped for a siesta like the Spanish, but the fear that the Comanches were watching them from every hill and tree drove them relentlessly on toward the fort.

Even Calhoun, who normally loved to talk, said little. Now and then his toothless gums would work a little, but he was talking to himself.

Mackenzie felt at times he might go mad. He could feel the sun cooking his brain. But there was no anodyne for the pain. It worsened until it seemed he could feel every bone in his body, from spine to heel, jar when he took a step.

On the third day they saw the fort. Mackenzie had had his Golgotha. He knew this agony was what Christ felt hanging there on the cross. But he held no forgiveness for his enemies; a burning desire for revenge rose like a blister in his heart. A blister that one day he would prick.

CHAPTER XIX THE WHITE RIVER

When Quanah, his band, and the fifty-odd saddle horses rode into the Quohadi camp on the White River headwaters of the Brazos, the camp grew ecstatic with the sure knowledge of how much the horses meant in terms of buffalo and in trade with other tribes.

Once each year, in early spring, the Quohadis drove a remuda of horses north to the Arkansas and there met a band of Ogallala Dakotas. In exchange for their horses, they got the beautiful red pipes carved from pipestone, beaver pelts, and the prized silver-tipped bearskins. The Dakotas only traded these bearskins in the spring, because it took a year to replace them. The Comanches then lugged the heavy skins, as well as buffalo hides, on their travois to each encampment throughout the year; but to face one winter in the driving blizzards and blue northers of the high plains, kept warm by a bearskin, was to realize its true, irreplaceable worth.

So Quanah's name spread among the Comanches. He was the young chief who had tweaked the nose of Mackenzie, the bluecoat leader who had uprooted Mowray's camp. The horses caused many more young Comanche maidens to gaze longingly at Quanah; among the Quohadi, the great chiefs had several wives, as was the custom. At present, Quanah had eyes only for Tonarcy. He might cast his eyes elsewhere when Tonarcy's belly was full and she must face the separation and confinement decreed by the old women for those near childbirth, but not until then.

As winter drew near, Quanah grew restless. Tonarcy sensed he wanted to go on another raid and urged him to do as his heart felt. "Go, my Quanah. My belly grows with our first child. Already you have many horses, but you give many away. Many of the old women told you they needed horses, and you gave. You are young and strong, and all the young warriors will follow. Take a war party and go punish our ancient foe, the Apache. Drive them further into the mountains of Mexico."

"*Aie*, Tonarcy! You read my thoughts. Have you too chewed on Father Peyote? He is the one who lets me read the thoughts of others. He is the one who calls me on this war party. Far to the south, in the mountains the Mexicans call the Chisos, I will find enough of Father Peyote to give and teach to all the Quohadis. Then, truly, our medicine power will be strong. If we go there, it is likely we will fight the Mescaleros."

"Go, my Quanah. Horse Back will tell you to go."

"I will go."

CHAPTER XX   A LEATHER QUIRT

Mackenzie found himself the butt of quite a few jokes back at Fort Concho. His outward composure was strict, firm, and unruffled; inwardly he seethed with humiliation. It took months before the pain and swelling in his leg subsided enough to let him stay in the saddle again. His reports to General Sherman at Fort Smith and to Colonel Miles at Fort Sill were scanty. The dispatch on the raid read,

> Encountered large band of Comanches fifty miles north. Lost sixty horses and mules in night encounter. Suffered only two casualties. Enemy casualties undetermined. Patrols continue daily. Replacement of horses hereby requested. Obediently, Ranald Mackenzie

The daily patrols went without Mackenzie now. Most frequently they went just a few miles from the fort, stayed within rifle shot, bivouaced for a few hours, and returned before nightfall. Calhoun knew the patrols were not really patrolling, but said nothing to Mackenzie.

To pass the time, Mackenzie braided a three-foot-long leather quirt for himself. He liked the sound of it when he struck his leather saddle boots. Often, a grim, vengeful smile would play across his face and then he would repeatedly snap the quirt against his boots. Occasionally the knob would graze his bad knee and the smile would twist into a grimace, but he quickly recovered. Mackenzie was training himself to control all his feelings. After a couple of months Calhoun, who had thought he knew Mackenzie well, found himself puzzled by his impersonal coldness.

When the fortunes of a man who has always tasted victory suddenly turn into a humiliating defeat, a subtle poison works on his mind until it galls him. Only the hope of revenge, a complete overwhelming vengeance, can soothe the irritation; when that thought came to Mackenzie, his thoughts turned inward, and no man knew him. He became a rattlesnake thrust into the rocks, coiled and ready to strike.

PHOTOGRAPHS

Quanah Parker in full Comanche regalia and holding a feather fan, seated next to an oil painting of his mother, Cynthia Ann Parker (Naduah), and sister, Prairie Flower (Topsanah). The photograph was probably taken at Fort Sill. Smithsonian Institution, Bureau of American Ethnology

Part of the Wilber S. Nye collection, this photographs shows Quanah in a full-length headdress, standing in front of a Comanche tepee. From *Plains Indian Raiders: The Final Phases of Warfare from the Arkansas to the Red River*, by Wilber Sturtevant Nye. Copyright 1968 by the University of Oklahoma Press.

Quanah Parker in war costume as he might have appeared during the battle of Adobe Walls. Smithsonian Institution, Bureau of American Ethnology

Colonel Ranald S. Mackenzie, 4th Cavalry, United States Army—Quanah's implacable adversary. U.S. Signal Corps Photo (Brady Collection), from *The Buffalo War* by James L. Haley, published by Doubleday and Company.

Quanah Parker and one of his wives; probably taken after he had been on the reservation for some time. Smithsonian Institution, Bureau of American Ethnology

Taken by Charles M. Bell of Washington, D.C., this view of Quanah Parker shows him dressed in a completely European fashion, down to umbrella and derby. Smithsonian Institution, Bureau of American Ethnology

Quanah Parker retained his long, tightly bound braids throughout his life. He is shown here at approximately age 64, still exhibiting the stern, proud visage that he possessed as a young Comanche warrior, master of the plains. Smithsonian Institution, Bureau of American Ethnology

photograph no. 57087

CHAPTER XXI   CHISOS MOUNTAINS

Quanah led a much larger band on this raiding party. Now, all the young braves insisted on riding with him, to share in his glory. Only those whom Horse Back asked to help protect the Quohadi camp stayed behind.

Quanah was not happy with the size of this war party. It would be almost impossible to steal across the staked plains and into the southern mountains unnoticed; it would make more difficult their mission, to find and pluck the peyote cactus from its stony bed.

If they met a band of Apaches or bluecoats, however, the extra warriors would be welcome. Nearly all carried their *bois d'arc* spears, the hard, orange wood polished to a high sheen. They were painted with red, yellow, and black designs, the serpent sign favored. The points were made from the heavy gray flint that was strewn along the upper Brazos and Colorado rivers. Quanah's spearpoint with its splashes of blue, red, and rich purple was of the beautiful, almost translucent Alibates flint from the Canadian River. This flint was exceedingly hard and took so long to work into a spearpoint the length of two hands that it was worth several horses. Ten Bears had given the point to Quanah as a way of protecting the guardian of his daughter.

As they rode south off the caprock onto the salt flats, Quanah headed slightly east to touch the big springs at the head of the

Conchos. It brought them dangerously close to his foe, Mackenzie, but they needed the water before striking south to the Pecos River. To protect his large party, Quanah strung it out in three groups: Lone Wolf and Otter Belt in a three-mile lead that gradually lengthened as they approached the plateaus and from which they could survey fifty miles in front of them; Quanah led the main band of seventeen warriors, strung out single file; and Red Horse and Iron Shirt brought up the rear, some two miles distant.

The land was familiar to most of the Comanches who rode almost yearly on raids, some deep into old Mexico. They regrouped on the mesas to rest their horses, chew on dried jerky, and wash small amounts of water down their dry throats. Endurance was their birthright; the long raid was like swimming a broad river whose distant shore is barely perceived. Their horses between their legs, they knew they would reach the other side and return.

In a week, they covered almost the length of Texas. At the blue-green waters of the bitter Pecos, they drank sparingly, but found plenty of small game to replenish their stores. Now they wound southwestward, deep into Apache territory. Mexican horses were not the prize on this raid. The small, rounded, stickerless humps of the peyote cactus were the goal of the hunt, and Quanah knew they grew in the Chisos, or bald mountains, near the great river.

This was Apache land. Comanches held the Apaches in almost as much contempt as they did the Pueblos to the west. The Apaches were superstitious and afraid to fight at night; they had never mastered the horse and the lance as had the Comanche. Nonetheless, they were fierce and, given the advantage of numbers and the knowledge of their own mountains, they would fight. But, the Chisos were holy lands, and Quanah knew the Apaches made no permanent camp there.

As they rode through the first pass that led into the mountains, Lone Wolf, who had already ridden to the top of the hill that skirted west of the pass, motioned them on. Quanah peaked the crest of the pass and rode through; the field-of-sight stunned his eyes. There before him, the mountains reeled like drunken clouds, piled fold on fold until they stretched away far below in Mexico.

Quanah's spirits lifted, as did his band's. A small burst of song sprang from his lips, and his men were deeply moved by it. To the plains Indians, who studied the sky as minutely as the land, such mountains could only bring them closer to the gods and the land of spirits in the blue heavens laid with clouds.

Quanah let his eyes reach; he was indeed farseeing, like his totem, Eagle. But even his eyes could not see past the seventh and last fold of mountains to tell him where land ended and sky began. All his senses were open—his ears heard the soft whistle of the wind through the pass, a hawk's cry; his nose picked up the sharp creosote smells of the desert floor beneath him.

They traveled slowly now, grouped closer together, but with more distance between each warrior. An enemy glimpsing them from afar would not be able to tell where the line of warriors started or stopped.

They crossed the dry streambeds of two little creeks and clambered over some low foothills. Marked for war, they were an imposing sight. No small band of Apaches would be likely to give them a fight. Just watching the ease with which they nudged their horses over the precipitous paths commanded respect.

Now they could see the Chisos in front of them, heaped together in a seemingly impenetrable castle of granite that threatened to leave the weak crumbling land, and with its upjut, vault into the more solid dome of heaven. The welcome green relief of the timbered slopes appeared among the crags now, and the Comanches' thoughts laced into one: deer.

In Quanah's mind, the peyote was uppermost, and he knew where he would find it—on the south rim where it fed on the sun. Rainstorms would have scoured the rocks clean, making it easy to locate.

They followed a dry streambed straight up into the mountains. The bright hues of the banded agate, jasper, and turquoise briefly caught their eyes. They knew how much their squaws would love and fondle these gems, and how much the Pueblos near Santa Fe would trade for the green and blue turquoise, but they knew, too, how worthless such stones would be if they cost a life.

Up in the pines the air was sweet. Their horses were quiet now; the pineleaf on the forest floor was broken by patches of bare rock or compacted dirt. From the slopes of the summits that came ever more near, the Comanches could see for hundreds of miles in all directions. Truly their chief, Quanah, was taking them up here to hold council with the gods themselves.

Quanah, in the lead now, remembered Doña Teresa's words: Father Peyote would be high but not too high, and on the southern exposure of the mountains. The Comanches were perturbed that Quanah now seemed to be leading them down out of the glorious mountains whose beauty they had tasted so briefly. His eyes searched the ground, and then he found them. They were not few or scarce as he had feared. They were many. They stood in their heaped-up little bulbs like small people, or tepees.

Quanah directed everyone to dismount quickly and gather as much peyote as they could pack in their small antelope tote bags. Otter Belt brought his first armload to Quanah who sat astride his gray spotted horse, his eyes darting everywhere. Quanah lay a hand of thanks on Otter Belt's arm and took the peyote from him. The other Comanches were surprised by the strange plant. A cactus without thorns must have great power to protect it from being eaten by animals. If this was the source of Quanah's power and medicine, then they would come to understand it and share it. Their bags full, once again they swung up on the backs of their horses.

Quanah now led them back up into the nests of the Chisos and made camp against huge granite boulders left from the dawn of time when the Chisos were much higher. He sent two hunting parties into the woods after deer, and stayed behind to commune with the spirits of the place in the company of a few of his old friends. Red Horse kept a sharp lookout from the top of the highest boulder.

The hunting parties were successful; four large mule deer provided the shoulders and backs the Comanches roasted over their campfires that night. They ate the livers and hearts raw. Some of the braves were eager to taste the peyote cactus, believing it to be like the *nopals* or pears of the prickly pear cactus, but Quanah forbade it. "Father Peyote must sit many moons in his own skin before he will let you chew on him." Many old stories of these hills and the mountains of Mexico were told and retold around the campfire. Each teller added bits of his own family and clan story to the larger story.

The lookouts kept a sharp watch, but the Comanches sensed that the Apache, if they were coming, were still far away. The holiness of the place would protect them. No one would attempt to climb the mountains at night. While the Comanches were warm in their Pueblo horse blankets, not a few of them longed for a buffalo robe or a bearskin to fend off the nippy air.

With the dawn, they arose and walked the stiffness out of their horses' legs before they mounted and followed Quanah down the southern slopes toward the Rio Grande. Many of the younger braves had never seen the great desert river that rolled so clear and green between the limestone and sandstone bluffs. Truly, it was as great as their Brazos River to the north.

The green willows and cottonwoods along the banks sheltered many animals. The black squirrels chattered, and high overhead, four golden eagles slowly circled down into the valley, their wings shining yellow when caught against the sun. The horses and men drank the fresh, sweet water slowly and deeply.

Quanah meant to follow the river east out of the mountains and then north to the Pecos and beyond. He cautioned that any hunting be done only with the silent bow. The Comanches, masters at concealing themselves in trees, stuck to the thickly wooded banks.

At one point, Iron Shirt rode back to tell Quanah of three Mexican families camped across the river. Quanah flashed the sign question for horses. No. Only burros and goats. Not enough to warrant a ride across the river in plain sight and the possible loss of a warrior, not when the Apaches surely lay ahead. The Mexican families never saw the Comanches in the thick willows, though their burros flicked their ears and flared their nostrils more than once.

As the mountains trailed more and more behind them, Quanah gave the signal to turn north away from the river after they had all filled their antelope flasks with its water. Quanah looked back to see the Sierra del Carmen wriggling like a giant snake in the sky, away into old Mexico as far as his eye could see. This sight would come often in his dreams, the last gift the mountain gods gave him.

CHAPTER XXII   MESCALERO APACHE

Perhaps they would not have seen the Apaches first if Quanah had not doubled the number of scouts on point, spreading them out like a fan in front of him. Lone Wolf, keenest of eye, saw them and folded the fan back up from his western flank. He guided Quanah and the entire band to a hill. There they saw clearly into the Apache camp.

The Apaches were in a dry arroyo that seemed to drop out of a flat plain, where the infrequent rains hit a softer gravel. They held a commanding view of the lower plains in front of them, pushing off to the east and south toward the river. Quanah made out a dozen horses, though only half that many warriors. Some might be asleep or resting in the deep shade of the bushes in the arroyo. More likely, the main body of men were off on a raid into Mexico. Nearly thirty women and children were in the camp, a large band for Apaches.

Quanah saw one sight that took his breath away: a young Apache maid just at the verge of womanhood. The litheness and suppleness of her body as she flitted through the camp stirred his male passion and added to the war passion which had been building within him.

He quickly laid out his plan, one which would take two or three painstaking hours to execute. Three warriors would dogleg south and, after waiting, would ride in plain sight up the arroyo as if they suspected nothing. Quanah and four of the best warriors—Iron

Shirt, Lone Wolf, Red Horse, and Ishtai, all of whom were known for their cunning—would circle to the north and come down the arroyo single file, walking their horses, out of sight. When the decoy drew near enough to the camp to properly distract them, the main force of the Comanches under Otter Belt would attack in a lightning charge from the hill. Quanah hoped this would panic the Apaches and cause them to flee through the creosote, ocotillo, and sawgrass to the east. Then, the killing would fall to the north force under him, which would be the closest. They would be better prepared, too, for an unfortunate return of the rest of the Apache band.

The plan worked better than he expected. The Apache sentry above the camp saw the three Comanche horsemen first, and ran swiftly into the camp to prepare the band for what seemed an easy ambush and easy pickings. Had older, wiser heads been in the camp, caution would have prevailed. The Apaches and Comanches had been mortal enemies for as long as either could remember; the old Mescaleros would know Comanches never came walking like blind rabbits into the stew pot, not the far-seeing Lords of the Plains.

When Otter Belt and his large band broke from the hill with their chilling war whoops, the Apaches saw that it was they who were trapped. What they did not know was how strong the jaws of the trap would be when it snapped shut. Like frightened rabbits, they flushed north and east through the low ground cover.

Quanah and his four long blades quickly leapt to their horses, their spears bristling in the sunlight. The Apache warriors, dimly aware of their newest peril, turned to fight, giving the women and children time to flee. Doom was written on their brows as they wheeled; their fierce and undimmed courage was also evident. They had no time to nock their arrows or raise their rifles before the Comanche spears worked their way of death.

Five Apache warriors fell almost as quickly as they rose to fight. The sixth leaped at Red Horse from the rear, his knife flashing. Red Horse knew he was there, and wheeled his horse accordingly. The long knife dug deep into his thigh, but missed his horse. His hatchet crashed glancingly on the Apache's skull and stayed him in his tracks, where Quanah's arrow pinned him in the dirt.

The Comanches turned now for the women and horses that had scattered like quail. Quanah had never lost sight of his other quarry. She was not hiding, but with blind faith in her quick legs, sprinted like an antelope for the blue hills. Because Quanah knew where she was, his horse beat the other Comanche braves to her.

Her long black hair flying, she never broke stride as Quanah's horse pounded close. He knew she would fight like a bobcat, and debated whether he should count coup on her and knock her out. He wanted no damaged goods, however, so he bent low, scooped her up around the waist, and rolled her onto her back in front of him. His free hand grabbed her hand with the knife as it flecked a bit of flesh from his ribs. He twisted the knife out of her hands and stunned her with a backhand slap. Then he rolled her over again, clasping both her hands behind her back in one large fist. She tried to drive her teeth into his knee, but a quick yank on her hair and Quanah's booming laughter made her lie still. For better or worse, her life now lay in the hands of this mighty giant who had captured her.

Seven other Comanches captured women. A dozen warriors caught up to the horses. With the other booty from the Apache camp, it was a major haul. The Comanches didn't scalp the fallen warriors. The women they caught might have been their wives; better for future peace to leave the Apaches where they had fallen.

As they rode the many days and nights toward their campgrounds high on the Canadian River, the Comanches were sure the peyote buds in their bags were protecting them and bringing good luck.

Mala, half Mexican, half Mescalero Apache, learned that Quanah was a gentle as well as a strong lover, and since she had never before been touched by a man, grew deeply attached to him by the time he dumped her in Tonarcy's lap and said, "Tonarcy is Quanah's first wife. You do as she says." Mala, happy as long as Quanah visited her bed regularly, did her chores as though she were Tonarcy's favorite younger sister. Tonarcy was secretly pleased to have her own Apache slave to do the hardest work, especially now that she was so heavy with child.

Quanah, when he gave any thought to the matter, concluded that the raid was successful. Red Horse suffered the only bad wound; it healed quickly, and, in stories by the campfires, Red Horse took great pleasure in telling how he came to have it. Quanah now had two beautiful wives, both more beautiful because they loved *him*. His beloved Tonarcy now had the great rolling curves of the buffalo, whereas the slender Mala had the slim, firm shape of the antelope. Both pleased him immensely. That fall, his first son was born.

CHAPTER XXIII THE WAGON RAID

Sherman had planned carefully for his Medicine Lodge Treaty Council. Runners had been sent to every tribe and band. Nearly all had come. Among the Comanche, only Quanah had refused to meet in the Medicine Lodge and talk. Quanah sent back the young Osage runner with this message: "Go tell General Sherman the Quchadis are warriors. If he wants our land, the bluecoats must first come and defeat us."

These words still galled Sherman three years later as his Indian policy crumbled into dust. True, most of the Cheyenne, Osage, Comanche, and Kiowa had come in on the reservations, but as long as there were buffalo to hunt and horses to steal, the reservation meant nothing to them.

Although many of the other chiefs had harsh words for the bluecoats at the Council, especially Horse Back, the promise of beef on the reservations overcame most of their qualms. However, as long as young wild chiefs like Quanah stayed off the reservation, the lure of that wild and free life remained strong.

The question was how to capture, kill, or break this Quanah. Sherman supposed he would have to turn Mackenzie loose with his "rabbit drives." That would be bad publicity, but the legal groundwork was now laid with the treaties setting aside the large reservations of land within Indian Territory. In the eyes of most white men, the army would be justified in pushing the various tribes onto lands set aside for them.

Fortune came to General Sherman the following spring. The Kiowa chiefs, Satanta, Satank, and Big Tree, led a small war party off the reservation at Fort Sill. They gravitated toward Fort Richardson, on the upper Brazos, to waylay the wagonloads of supplies headed that way. Sherman himself, with a small escort of less than a dozen soldiers, passed along the hill under the scheming eyes of Satanta and the others. They would have fallen on them and made short work of them, but Satanta thought there was not enough booty in Sherman's entourage. His preference for traveling light had saved the general.

The Kiowas waited until three long wagons, headed by six mules each and loaded with every sort of ration, swung beneath the hill. The muleteers never knew what hit them.

Ordinarily Satanta would have made good his escape, melting into the cross timbers and across the Red River into Oklahoma. This time, the fates would have it otherwise. Another wagonmaster happened along within the hour and hauled the mutilated and scalped bodies of the muleteers into Fort Richardson for Sherman's inspection.

Mackenzie was there, too, for a conference with Sherman. In the hot afternoon sun, he watched Sherman's nearly bald head turn beet red as he examined the bodies: the few bristly hairs on the back of his neck stiffened in both fear and anger as he realized how easily his scalp might have been lifted on the same trail.

"Ranald, I want you to take as many men as you need. Trail those renegades to the Canadian border if you have to, and bring them back here for trial. Those eighteen shod army mules should leave you a pretty good trail."

"You mean a military trial, sir?"

"No, we'll let these Texans try them in *their* courts."

"These are Kiowa shafts, sir. Likely, they will beeline it to Fort Sill and under Kicking Bird's wing."

"Mackenzie, find out who they are. Bribe, torture, or kill a few. I want the leaders back here, even if it's Kicking Bird himself."

"Aye, aye, sir!" And the tall colonel strode away on his game leg, a twisted, evil grin splitting his face. By God, he thought, we've got some of those red bastards now.

Mackenzie followed the Indians' trail with a full company. If he had pressed his men he might have caught up with the Kiowas on the trail, but he wanted to implicate every Indian on the reservation. Even at that, he probably would have failed to bring anyone back, had it not been for the clever tongue and the shrewd ideas of the Quaker missionary, Tatum, who ran the reservation for the Secretary of the Interior.

Tatum had already heard via his grapevine which chiefs had led the raid, so he sent for Satanta, Satank, and Big Tree to interview them in Mackenzie's presence. These were real troublemakers, and he thought by throwing these bones to the army's wolf—young Mackenzie—it would leave him with a free hand to run the reservation.

Bluecoated soldiers lined the walls of Tatum's hand-hewn log office. Mackenzie stood patiently in a corner of the room. The Kiowa chiefs bristled with fury, since they rightly suspected some squirrel had uncovered their stolen nuts. "Satanta," Tatum's preaching voice boomed out, "the Comanches tell me it was them and not the Kiowas who stole nearly twenty army mules eight days ago in Texas."

Satanta could not stand this personal affront to his pride and glory, and he saw not the lying tongue of Tatum. "The Comanches lie. I stole those mules." Tatum rejoined, "But Big Tree shot the army wagonmaster and killed him." Satanta, now in a rage, could not be restrained by Satank and Big Tree, who were trying to shut him up.

"No! I drew my bow—like this—and shot dead the wagon man. We took their scalps, all of them."

This was enough for Mackenzie, and he motioned for his men to take the three chiefs. After a fierce grapple, they were under control. Mackenzie had his prey now, and he began the trip back to Texas, the Indians in bonds.

As they traveled along the road, if the bluecoats had known Kiowa, they would have known Satank was singing his death song in the back of the open wagon. He slipped the ropes off his arms, feet, and legs, and leaped for one of the bluecoats riding alongside the wagon, pulling him to the ground. Two rifles began to pour lead into Satank as soon as he stood upright. What amazed the soldiers was how long he stood after he was shot. His death song finished as he died. They buried him there in the dirt, beside the road, with no marker. The young soldier returned to his place beside the wagon, frightened but wiser.

At Jacksboro, Sherman turned the two chiefs over to the local sheriff and judge for trial. Though Mackenzie would dearly have loved to hang the Indians himself, for once he thought Sherman was right. A young lawyer, W. T. Lanham, prosecuted the two Kiowa chiefs, and made a reputation that later helped him become elected governor. His best witness was Colonel Ranald Mackenzie, who described vividly Satanta's admissions at Fort Sill, and went into great detail about the general "Indian problem" on the whole frontier.

Big Tree and Satanta were sentenced to be hung, and sent to the state prison at Huntsville to await execution. A wave of protests around the country, especially among Quakers who were not happy with Tatum's duplicity in catching the Indians, caused President Grant to intervene and request clemency for the two Kiowa chiefs from the Texas governor. The governor granted his request, changing their sentence to life imprisonment. Big Tree was to die leaping from a prison roof top, trying to escape. Satanta was later paroled and died in the company of his old comrade-in-arms, Quanah.

CHAPTER XXIV DOUBLE MOUNTAIN

Sherman moved Mackenzie to Fort Griffin on the Brazos, with an outpost at Fort Phantom Hill (near where the town of Abilene would eventually form). He also gave Mackenzie the green light for his "rabbit drives."

"Sweep Texas clean of Indians. To the Red River. Beat the bushes and the river bottoms. Capture or kill every manjack Comanche you find. There's room for them all at Fort Sill. Also, make available free arms and ammunition to the buffalo hunters working out of Fort Griffin. If we get the buffalo, we'll get the Indian."

Mackenzie was pleased with his orders. Despite the increased patrols, however, the Comanche horse raids continued. Mackenzie knew someday he would have to track the Comanche serpent to his den on the high plains and put a finish to him there. He wondered if that would be where fate brought Quanah before his eyes again.

The pressure on the buffalo herds was beginning to tell on the Comanches. Northern hunters operating out of Laramie and Kearny decimated the buffalo's numbers. The Comanches were turning now toward the Texas ranchers, not only for horses but for cattle as well. The easiest pickings were from the trail herds driven each spring to the railheads in Kansas.

As the small towns peppered westward on the Kansas plains, the Texas cattlemen swung the Chisholm trail westward to catch the sweet prairie grass and the sweet dollars of the cattle buyers sooner. Most drives stayed west of the Brazos until Fort Worth or Granbury. Just south of Granbury at Mitchell Bend, a shelf of limestone rock afforded an ideal place to cross wagons; north of Granbury between Rock Bluff and Cedar Bluff lay one of the best hard-gravel fords, one that never washed out. Few cattle were lost to the treacherous Brazos River quicksands at these two crossings.

With the sprinkling of forts further west, however, and the increased patrols, some hardy cattlemen could swing wide on the western prairie, avoiding the heavy forests of the cross timbers. There were many little rivers to cross—the Lampasas, the Bosque, the Leon, and the Paluxy—but for the most part they had limestone floors, and ran shallow except at floodtime.

Jack Thorp and Walter Blevins were trailing their herds together the spring of '73 for safety, and swung wide, hoping to catch the Brazos where it had already branched into the Clear, Salt, and Double Mountain forks, making easy crossing on all three. They had been told to look out for the Double Mountain caprock northeast of Fort Phantom Hill, which sat on the ground like an eagle with outstretched wings.

Ten days out of Waco they saw it, and were impressed as they moved toward it. It was a two-headed mountain, with one escarpment rearing to the east, one to the west; they swerved to the west side to cross the river. Quanah and his band of warriors watched them from the top of the mountain.

It was dusk when they reached the river, and it was full with spring rains. They quickly decided to water the herd and cross them in the morning at first light. After they had bedded the cows down, and stuck Bob Cartwright and Big John Killough on first watch, they gathered around the mesquite campfire to eat pinto beans, cooked in the big black kettle and sprinkled liberally with dried pork sides, red and black peppers, and chunks of fresh beef, killed when one of the cows broke its leg by stepping in a prairie dog hole. The hardtack cornbread, which had made many a cowboy snaggle-toothed, softened in the thick bean soup.

After supper the cowboys who hadn't already caved in to sleep were hungry for music and turned to Hugh Thomason, and his French harp. Hugh sang them one of the sad cowboy songs about a lost love called *The Rivers of Texas*. As the song ended, many a cowhand was hurrying to those green pastures of sleep, to dream of the loved one they had left behind or the loved one they hoped someday to find. Thomason hummed a few more verses in a quiet tone, rolled himself a final smoke, settled into his blankets, and feasted his eyes on the eternal river of light called the Milky Way.

Out over the prairie, Cartwright and Killough took turns repeating the verses of the river song until they had sung it out, then started in on other familiar tunes like *Little Joe The Wrangler,* or *The Wild Spanish Bull.* As alert as they were, they were unprepared for the Comanche whirlwind that scattered their herd.

Quanah had planned it carefully. Able to think like the cattlemen, he knew the cowboys would stick with the main part of the herd. Thus he would hit from the west, driving the bulk of the herd into the draw between the two mountains, heavily timbered with scrub cedar and live oaks. His other band would attack up from the river and slice off twenty to thirty head. He had sent Otter Belt on foot down the steep southern slope of the mountain to build up a bonfire hedge which would help spook the herd, and at the right moment, turn them up the draw. Otter Belt would then hide out in a cave known only to a few Comanches, and Quanah would return the next evening with a spare horse to pick him up.

The clear sky clouded up close to midnight and a few distant rumbles of thunder set the cows on edge. Cartwright and Killough had just ridden into camp to wake their reliefs when the Comanches struck. The herd started moving when they heard the shots and piercing yells from the Comanches. Otter Belt had nurtured his dry-stick fire well. When he ignited the rolled tumbleweeds and dry cedar limbs, they flared and lit the drama with a stunning blaze. The main body of the herd poured up the draw.

With the cowboys jumping and scrabbling for their horses in the darkness, the Comanches made a clean getaway to the west with close to forty head, nearly four times the number they might have stolen by stealth alone.

Thorp was cussing a blue streak. Blevins bellowed out orders quickly. "Stay with the herd, men. Fire only when you can put some daylight through these marauders. Head the herd off and turn them. Don't let them reach the river!"

When daybreak shed some light on their predicament, the cowhands were able to make better sense of what they had to do. It took them half a day to gather the herd. Two hands, Killough and Strickland, were killed in the stampede. They were buried there in the shadow of the fateful Double Mountain, with only boards ripped from the side of the chuck wagon to mark the mounds of rocks that were their graves.

Thorp and Blevins decided to head due east to Fort Griffin, and to get the bluecoats on the trail of the Comanches. They didn't have enough men to start a pursuit themselves. Then, too, they hoped to pick up an army escort going at least as far as Fort Sill. It would cost a few more beeves, but it would be worth it, given what they lost and stood to lose, should the raid be repeated.

When morning came, Quanah, his band, and the stolen cattle were thirty miles to the west. From a low mesa, he could tell they were not being followed. He placed Ishtai as chief in his place to herd the cows up onto the caprock where his hungry women and children were encamped. Taking one of the fastest horses, he swung far south to return and pick up Otter Belt, his faithful friend, whose bonfire sealed the success of their raid. To conceal himself, he moved slowly and very cautiously, sticking to the drywater draws.

At Fort Griffin, Mackenzie, Calhoun, and his staff were glad to see the traildrivers, for no other reason than they stirred things up. Men could hit the saddle with plausible excuse. Things had been too quiet lately.

Mackenzie and a large patrol would accompany the cowboys and their herd north to Fort Sill. Lieutenant Allen and forty men were already heading west to trail and try to capture the cattle thieves. Mackenzie doubted he would have the luck this time of tracking the stolen livestock right to the reservation. These animals were stolen by some hungry wolves up on the plains.

Two Tonkawa scouts were out well ahead of the patrol. They arrived at Double Mountain with an hour of daylight. Skirting the mountain to the south, they came upon the remnants of the camp, the two graves, and debris left in the confusion. Riding then toward the mountain, they were puzzled by the signs of the big bonfire. The sharp-eyed Tonkawas dismounted and went very slowly.

Otter Belt had dusted away his tracks with a large cedar limb, but in the darkness had missed some, and the cedar switch had left its own faint tracks back to a dry spring bed on the side of the mountain. The chief Tonkawa scout, Talpah, motioned to the other to hold his horse while he explored on foot.

To his trained eye, a very dark patch of juniper midway up the mountain looked suspicious. Nowhere else did the salt cedars cluster that thickly. He went straight up, approaching the spot where Otter Belt lay hidden from a lateral side. His army Colt pistol was drawn and cocked.

The sound of the cocking of the pistol alerted Otter Belt. Too close in the cave for his bow, and he did not have his lance with him. He must rely on his knife. He drew himself up in a crouch ready to spring.

When Talpah, the mortal foe of the Comanche, drew back the thick juniper to reveal the face of the cave, Otter Belt leaped. Had he had his spear, the match would have been uneven. As it was, Talpah's Colt bucked and roared, and Otter Belt tumbled to the side, his knife harmlessly grazing Talpah's knuckles. Talpah took his own knife, lifted the Comanche's scalplock, seized his weapons, and went back down to his excited compadre. They now had a prize to show Colonel Mackenzie and Lieutenant Allen. They would tell Allen the Comanches' trail was cold, and Allen would be glad enough to turn back toward the fort.

Quanah was still a long way from the mountain near dusk, when a hot sharp pain like a wave of sheet lightning swept through his mind. In his mind's eye and with his mind's ear, he heard Otter Belt's death cry and felt the heat of Otter Belt's death fury. He sped his horse into a full gallop toward the mountain, but his heart was heavy as lead within. With whatever surge of spirit Otter Belt had cried out to him, that spirit was now departed. Otter Belt's soul was lost in the spirit world.

It was past dark when Quanah led the horses into the cover of the cedars, tied them, and scrambled up quickly toward the cave. Otter Belt lay where the Tonkawa had left him. From the way the scalp was taken, Quanah guessed it was a Tonkawa. He ran his hand over the large hole where the shell had come out of Otter Belt's back. The Tonkawa snake had the white man's pistol; otherwise he would be here instead of Otter Belt. Quanah's heart was very hot inside his chest; he felt his hate for the Tonkawa plunge into the lake of his hatred for the white soldiers and emerge doubly hot.

He quietly shouldered Otter Belt's body, already stiff, and carried it down to the horses. The body was heavy, but Quanah in his rage was numb to its weight. Back at the village in the Palo Duro, there would be much weeping and wailing. Otter Belt was a stalwart of his tribe and would be sorely missed. He would be buried with his weapons in a cave in the walls of the Palo Duro. Quanah must take his two wives under his own tent, for it was his order that had kept Otter Belt behind. Such was the Comanche way; one took care of the living to show care for the dead.

CHAPTER XXV   MEDICINE CHIEF

At this time in the Comanche camp there was a need and a demand for new medicine. The old medicine chief, Towap, had died. Quanah had so far refused the use of the peyote buds because he knew they had not seasoned like the Mexican *curandero* had told him they must. Too, Quanah was reluctant to take on the role of medicine chief since he was being groomed to be war chief after Horse Back, and the Comanches traditionally kept the roles separate.

Ishtai had a falling out with Quanah. Ishtai begged Quanah to let the whole council partake of the peyote, and Quanah refused. "When we have a new medicine chief," Quanah said, "then I will show him Father Peyote, and he will decide." Ishtai went away very bitter, and Quanah was not too puzzled at his old friend. The Comanches were used to having a medicine chief, a seer, whose visions warned them of impinging danger, as well as helped to provide food. With the bluecoats pressing more closely on their traditional lands, all the Comanches, Quanah not excepted, felt the need for new and strong medicine.

Quanah was not surprised when Ishtai started having visions and reporting them to the men in the tribe at their evening council fire. Perhaps Ishtai was using the peyote against Quanah's command, perhaps not. Quanah had his doubts and suspicions however, especially in light of the fragmentary nature of Ishtai's visions.

Ishtai was having very powerful dreams, but no one could interpret them. He said he saw a great brown and red spider wrap its legs around the Comanche lodges, and they disappeared. Then he would dream of an enormous pile of bones that reached to the heavens, but when asked whether the bones were those of the Comanche or of their enemies, he wouldn't say. Ishtai would in no way interpret his dreams, but he let hints slip out that when he did interpret his dreams, his power would have filled his cup full.

Ishtai was painting half of his face and his body blue, the traditional colors of the medicine chief. On his blue chest he would paint a yellow sun, moon, and stars to show he was walking in the spirit world. When he painted his whole face and body blue, he hinted, then his medicine gourd would be full.

Tonarcy was deeply disturbed both by Ishtai's growing power and by how much it upset Quanah. She would try to console Quanah as she suckled their young boy, Tonopah, as they sat with Quanah's three other wives around the fire eating their supper. None of the Comanches liked the beef as well as buffalo, but ate it without complaint.

"Quanah, Ishtai is jealous of your power, is he not?"

"I think not. Ishtai and I are friends."

"But he was with you when you tricked Mackenzie. He saw your power, and now he wants this same power as yours."

"That may be, Tonarcy. But we must wait. When Ishtai's medicine gourd is full, then he will interpret his dreams. If I challenge his right to be medicine chief, I must do it then in full council. But till then I must keep silent. Ishtai is truly walking in the spirit world. What he has to tell us from his dreams may save our people."

Tonarcy was silent, but her heart still beat fast within her. She was glad for her new sisters, these new wives of Quanah. Otter Belt's wives had long been among her best friends. Even Mala had lost her reserve, and did as Tonarcy bid her around the camp. Tonarcy hoped Quanah was filling them with sons, since she sensed someday the Comanches might have to fight to the death with the bluecoated whites who were encroaching on their lands. She knew Quanah's white blood gave him knowledge and power over the whites, a power Ishtai could never match.

Mala was contented. She had come to love Tonarcy as she loved Quanah, and the fierce pride of the Comanches filled her breast. She felt Quanah's child stirring within her, but would tell him only when she could no longer conceal it. She wanted her tall, strong chief to keep visiting her at night, and always slept naked between her buffalo robes to be ready for him. She did not quite understand all this spirit talk. The Comanches had more gods than the Apaches and worshipped them in different ways, though some gods were the same, like Father Coyote. She knew that if Quanah knew Father Peyote, then he was as cunning as the Tarahumaras in Chihuahua, that he could appear at his enemies' campfire and disappear at will. She folded her dream of Quanah around her like a blanket until early morning, when dream became reality. Then her lithe body sang like a meadowlark.

CHAPTER XXVI ISHTAI'S MEDICINE

Ishtai's dream was complete. He had dreamt it now twelve times. At the council fire, he was painted blue from head to toe. The speckles of yellow in the blue glittered in the firelight. He looked like the strangest vision anyone could hope to have, which added to his power. Horse Back, Quanah, and the others waited patiently for him to bring forth his medicine.

Ishtai spoke slowly and carefully. "My medicine gourd is full. The vision has come twelve times now; each time I saw and heard more clearly what my medicine spirit told me. The valley of bones are our buffalo. Each year, now, the buffalo hunters come with their wagons and slay our buffalo only for the hides. Each summer the buffalo are fewer. Where once they surged like a mighty river up and down the prairie, now they are but a trickle."

Horse Back was deeply moved by Ishtai's statement. "What then would you have us do, Ishtai? How can we restore the buffalo in its numbers to our high plains?"

"We must kill all the buffalo hunters. Already they gather at Fort Griffin. My friends, the crows, tell me they are already returning to their old trading post at Adobe Walls, so near to us that were I an eagle"—and he glanced at Quanah—"I could spit on them."

Horse Back was startled by this new information. "The Adobe Walls on the creek where we drove the mighty Carson and his warriors like quail before the wind?"

"The same Adobe Walls in the heart of buffalo country."

"*Aiiee!* We nearly lifted Carson's hair from his head that time. He left over half his men, nearly forty, when he fled." Horse Back's face grew very animated in retelling this old battle. He then looked piercingly at Ishtai and said, "Tell us, Ishtai. If this be true, when and how shall we attack these buffalo hunters?"

Ishtai was cautious now. He added a few buffalo chips to the fire. "First, there must be a great gathering of the tribes. The Quohadi Comanche must be joined by the buffalo clan, the Coth-cho-tekas, the wasp clan, the Pena-tekas, the Kiowas, the Kiowa-Apache, and the southern Cheyenne if they will come."

"Why so many warriors, Ishtai? Surely, the buffalo hunters are not so many."

"We must strike terror in the hearts of the white men along the whole frontier. When they learn we gather in such numbers, they will not dare come across our hunting lands."

This answer pleased Horse Back. He turned now to Quanah. "What says Quanah? Is this not a good plan? Ishtai sees far in his vision. Shall we not wipe out the buffalo hunters?"

Quanah spoke slowly and carefully, yet with all the authority he could muster. "Ishtai speaks well. I agree. We should call a great war party of all the Comanches. Let the Kiowa come if they wish. A war party like the one that drove the Apache forever into the southern mountains, or the one raised against the Tejanos after their treachery in the courthouse at San Antonio. But we should strike, not against the buffalo hunters, but here at Fort Griffin against the bluecoats themselves. Drive the hound from our midst, and he will carry his fleas with him!"

The whole council was stirred by Quanah's bold speech. The elders and warriors were muttering to each other about it.

Horse Back was puzzled, however. This was the first he had heard of Quanah's proposed strike against one of the bluecoats' forts. "Tell us more, Quanah. What spirit has spoken to you, and where is your medicine?"

"The bluecoats aim to drive us from our lands and pen us like cattle. All of you know Comanche and Kiowa who eat from their hand at Fort Sill. Red Cloud and the Ogallalas defeated the bluecoats in open battle. A small war party could draw the bluecoats from their walls, and the great war party could fall on them in the breaks and canyons of the Brazos. If we do not fight them there on our day, then sometime we must fight them here on their day."

Horse Back mused long over this. He knew there was much

to Quanah's plan, but that he had not completely thought it out. "What does Quanah say then, if we gather the tribes and all the warriors, and attack the buffalo hunters first as Ishtai says, then go from there and drive the bluecoats from their fort."

Quanah saw Horse Back was committed to Ishtai's plan. "Then let it be as you say. We will follow Ishtai's medicine for now. Call the warriors. Let us strike the buffalo scavengers in their sleep!"

CHAPTER XXVII — ADOBE WALLS

The Harris and Taylor Fur Company in St. Louis had been buying furs from the mountain men for sixty years. The easiest drive was over the southern plains to the yearly rendezvous at Taos north of Santa Fe. Other furs came down the great broad back of the Missouri. From St. Louis, the furs went to New Orleans, New York, and all the capitals of the world. With the reoccupying of the Union forts after the Civil War, the fur traders became more aggressive and posted trading posts ever deeper into Indian Territory.

The beaver were almost gone, trapped out; the various western streams now ran to their home in the sea, unimpeded by beaver dams. The fur companies sold the idea of the buffalo robe; greater demand from Europe and the cities of the east spurred the buffalo slaughter.

A trader named Hanrahan had reoccupied Adobe Walls the summer of 1873, trading supplies to the hunters on the south plains. He made plans to rendezvous with all of the hunters by the Ides of March the following spring, to get an even earlier start.

The crowd that gathered there at Adobe Walls that fateful spring included names already famous on the frontier: men like Bat Masterson, who had laid more than a handful of crooked card dealers to rest in Abilene and other cattle towns; Ben Tilghman, a former

Texas Ranger known to many; others, like young Billy Dixon, would make their fame in the days to come. Dixon hung out with the half-breed, Amos Jackman, whose mother was Comanche, married to a white settler near Weatherford. There were Jackson and Slaughter, and a dozen other ex-cowboys who had learned they could make ten times in a summer skinning buffaloes what they made all year as a cowhand.

Some had been in camp more than a week, waiting for the weather to break. Entertainment was provided by Sally Flowers, the red-headed Irish peach with a fair singing voice, wife of Hanrahan's assistant, and a tall, lanky, gray-headed cowboy named Bill Philips who knew every song yet written on the American frontier.

Hanrahan and Flowers had carted in enough ten-foot cedar poles and piñon pine logs to build a stockade around the three adobe-walled buildings. Two brothers from Santa Fe, the Sadlers, had some claim to one of the buildings, so it was serving as the saloon, hotel, and eating place for the hunters. The Sadlers had packed in a big wood-burning stove with a dutch oven all the way from St. Louis. They quickly hired Sally Flowers as cook, for men in a primitive wilderness would sooner eat food cooked by a woman than any other vittles.

While the men were enjoying the company and the camaraderie of the other hunters, they were getting restless. Most had invested all they had in supplies and were anxious to get out and start skinning buffaloes. They were armed to the ears with four or five rifles apiece: the traditional .50 caliber Sharps buffalo gun, the new '73 model Winchester repeating rifles, and Colt pistols they had received along with free ammunition from Mackenzie's supply sergeant at Fort Griffin. With the big Sharps, a buffalo hunter could conceal himself well over a half mile away from the buffalo and plunk into the herd all day, without the other buffalo becoming alarmed by the steady boom of the rifle.

It was a cold blustery night. The wind had howled down out of the Canadian wastes for four days now. Many of the men were hopeful the blizzard would let up and allow them to start out the following day. Not a few already had their card sense sharpened playing poker with Masterson, and he was having trouble scraping together even a small-ante poker game. Everyone feasted on Sally Flowers' hearty beef stew and homemade tortillas, fried Mexican style. Now they laid back on the rough-hewn chairs and tables, unlimbering their tobacco and talking quietly about their prospects for the spring, the wind, the Indians, the price of hides, and the thousand tales each had heard of men matching their wits against their wild prairies.

Masterson baited young Billy Dixon a bit. "You're not going hunting with that Indian, are you, boy?" Jackman, while dressed as the frontiersmen, had his traditional black braids down his back. "Don't you know the game? We hunt the buffalo, the Comanche hunts us. That 'breed will lead them right to you, boy."

"Well, Amos and me got a deal made. I shoot the buffalo and he skins them."

This joke brought a grunt from the taciturn Amos. "Humph! Amos shoot his own buffalo. Dixon lucky to hunt with me. I show him where many buffalo wallow."

Masterson blew his smoke in Jackman's face now. "Whatcha gonna do when Quanah Parker swoops down on you, Jackman? You gonna tell him you're half red man, too? Maybe he will take you back into his tribe."

"Nope. Amos gonna be like white man with Quanah. With this hand I lift up and say, 'Peace!' and with my other hand I reach for my army Colt pistol!"

This brought huge guffaws from the hunters. None caught the irony in Jackman's voice, an irony honed sharp by living in two worlds, the red man's and the white.

Philips hauled out his French harp and guitar and ran a few introductory chords and notes. Even Sally Flowers' face, tired and worn from her chores, brightened into a smile.

Philips was tall, about 6'4", with grizzled hair for a young man—he had experienced a few hair-raising adventures. He trapped beaver with mountain men in Wyoming and Utah, made the yearly rendezvous at Taos, and even cowboyed down in Texas with old man Goodnight, after meeting him in Santa Fe. More than a few Indian women had warmed his bed when occasion permitted.

"Boys, here's a buffalo-hunting song I heard. Whether it's so, I don't know. But it's about not having enough grubstake to go on—'going short'—and like some of us could honestly testify, sometimes our own pocket money runs mighty low. Now this fellow, Griego, in the song, is the name you hear in New Mexico. In Texas I've sometimes heard the name Innis"—this perked up several ears—"but it's a good song called *The Home* or *The Range of the Buffalo*." He strummed the guitar and began to sing.

>Come all you buffalo hunters and listen to my song.
>You needn't get uneasy, for it isn't very long.

> It's concerning some buffalo hunters who all agreed
> to go
> And spend a summer working, among the buffalo . . .

Philips continued, singing of the promises and flattery used to attract hunters, and then of the miserable conditions the men encountered. The nods, grunts of approval, and volleys of applause told Philips the song rang true with these men, some of whom had skinned buffaloes for four or five seasons. He continued.

> When the summer at last ended old Griego began
> to say
> My boys you've been extravagant, so I'm in debt today.
> But among the buffalo hunters bankrupt law don't go
> So we left old Griego's bones to bleach among the
> buffalo.
>
> Now we're back across Pease River and homeward
> we are bound
> In that forsaken country may I never more be found.
> If you see anyone bound out there pray warn them
> not to go
> To that forsaken country, the land of the buffalo.

As he finished, there were shouts from the men sprawled around the room. "Another one! Sing some more, hell, we ain't tired!"

Philips then drew out his French harp, laying down the melody for the trail-driving song, the *Goodnight-Loving Trail*. When he hit lines like "It's a wonder the wind don't tear off your skin, get in there and blow out the light," one could hear the exclamations of appreciation. When he was through chanting the song of the chuck-wagon widow, more than half the hunters were asleep. Like cows or little children, their hearts had opened to this particular mournful tune and it had transported them.

Philips quietly ran through a few more familiar tunes on the harmonica, then rolled himself up in a faded grizzly-bear hide and slept.

Sally Flowers, as she curled up in her husband's arms in their bunk behind the bar, said—a bit to his embarassment—"My, can't that cowboy sing! I'd like to take him home with me. Wouldn't you, Shug?"

Out of the night came a laconic "Hun-uh. Let's sleep."

Tilghman was one of the last to turn in, and he chose a wide bench piled with blankets right under the main crossbeam of the building. He somehow didn't quite trust the half-breed and wanted to be where he could watch him go to sleep in the dim candlelight.

By midnight, the place was filled with snores. Hard men who live hard lives give up the ghost when they go to sleep, and often snore vigorously; a team of men sawing logs is a fair comparison.

Something was troubling Tilghman's sleep, however. As a boy he had always been told he had the gift of second sight by the older womenfolk. Not ever bothering to find out what "second sight" meant, he trusted the premonitions that came to him. Somewhere in his dreams he felt a great turbulence, like a buffalo stampede or a large number of horses running headlong.

So, he was almost awake when he heard the timber creaking above his head. As he crossed that thin threshold into wakefulness, his hand slid down and loosed from its holster the big Colt .44. Whether it was the wind creaking the timbers, or the roofbeam about to give out, Tilghman didn't know. He was certain someone was on the roof trying to get in. "Injuns" was his only thought. And Comanches would be the only ones to attack at night. He tried to guess from the creaking just where the varmints lay. The crashing of the broken crossbeam and the roar of the Colt restored life to all those sleeping logs, and the cabin was a hubbub of men shouting, loading rifles, cocking pistols, and yelling.

"Light, light, light a candle!"

The whirlabub lessened when men could see. Then they were all ashamed of having been so scared, and thankful they hadn't shot one another. "What happened, Ben? What did you shoot at?"

"Boys, I thought sure it was an Injun on the roof who broke that crossbeam, but all I find on the floor is a feather."

"Whoo-hah! A feather! Ben, you can't make a living skinning birds, it's buffalo we're after!"

Tilghman was considerably embarassed. Now he spoke out of the depth of the feeling that had awakened him. "I could have been mistaken about that roof; this beam's pretty well rotted, and it could have been breaking, or my slug might have snapped it. But something woke me up. I got a feeling we're in grave danger, and it's Injuns if you ask me."

This assertiveness loosened the half-breed Amos's tongue. "Tilghman is right. Many voices in the wind tonight. Amos could not sleep." The mood in the room grew darker. These two men were giving voice to every man's fear. Hanrahan spoke next. "Well, it's getting on toward daylight, I reckon. No need to try and sleep now.

I've got an extra jar of good whiskey somewheres, which, with some coffee, will warm us up. Come daybreak, the Sadlers can take a team down to the creek and get a couple of cottonwood beams. Philips, where's that guitar? I sure hope it ain't busted."

"Nope, sure ain't. I'm the only one here that's unstrung. Maybe some playing will tie me back together again."

The gloom quickly turned into cheer. Tilghman was still giving a lot of black looks, and no one quite looked him in the eyes, though Masterson was studying him close from the corner of his eye. Billy Dixon huddled in a corner with Amos, trying to get him to say more about his sleeplessness, and now Dixon's face was clouded by a dark look.

At first gray light of dawn, the two Sadler brothers hitched a horse to the small open wagon and were let out the stockade gate. They each took a rifle, but grabbed only what lay at hand, single shot .50 caliber Sharps. Dan lay his rifle under his feet while he held the reins, and Burke carried his at the ready.

The wind had ebbed somewhat, but was stiff in the Sadlers' faces as they rolled the wagon down the gentle slope to the creek. The tall, thigh-deep grasses rustled as they yielded before the gusts. It was light enough to see now, with a few faint cracks of red shimmering in the eastern sky.

As Dan and Burke beheld the running tide of doom, Dan unconsciously reined the horse to a halt. Here was a sight if there ever was one.

Somewhere between seven hundred and a thousand Comanches and Kiowas in full battle headdress bore down on them in an all-out gallop from the north. The din of hooves roared in their heads, and their blood pounded like thunder. They could even hear the silky whistling of thousands of feathers as the Comanches, like birds of prey, swooped down.

Burke squeezed off one shot; where it went, he never knew nor lived to tell. The Comanche horde split in waves around the wagon. Comanche spears dipped and picked the Sadlers out of their seats like bacon forked from the pan. By the time the horses had ridden over, there was barely enough left to tell that these were men and not rag dolls.

The shot electrified the men inside the stockade. The gate was barred. Masterson and Tilghman moved like whirlwinds, rolling wagons behind the gate, laying out boxes of ammunition and extra rifles for every man. Their natural leadership rose like cork, and the others obeyed.

Billy Dixon stood stock-still and watched the Comanches come. Amos fetched his Sharps and a Winchester repeater. Years later he would tell his children and their children that "he had seen the Comanche in all his glory." There have been but few sights in the annals of the American frontier to equal the battle charge that swept down on the buffalo hunters at Adobe Walls.

Horse Back, Quanah, Kicking Bird, Lone Wolf, and other chiefs led, their eagle-feather headdresses, which reached to their knees, snaking backwards in the flow of the wind. The Indians rode low on their mounts, giving the horses a winged appearance. Their spears and rifles were held at the ready, their bows and arrows slung on their backs. They knew the single shot had spoiled their surprise, but their fury drove them on. The blood of the two skinners would not slake even one Comanche's thirst when they were in this war mood.

Masterson kept yelling at the hunters to hold their fire until they were closer. He knew how hard it was to hit an Indian on horseback. Now the Comanches were upon them. The noise of the hooves, the spectacle of feathers and warpaint created a thick chock of fear in the back of each man's throat.

Quanah drove his horse on. He knew how many rifles were behind those walls. Why did they not bark? Was Ishtai's medicine this strong? Would they yet surprise the white buffalo hunters?

Then the first volley broke from the cedar stockade. Men and horses went down in clouds. More Comanche and Kiowa kept coming. The horde broke and split around the stockade that shielded the three small adobes. Their spears thudded into the walls and the ground like giant arrows hurled from the sky. But the Comanche fury was misspent; their targets were sheltered by the stout logs. Only a few nicks and yelps of pain were heard.

The Comanches regrouped on the other side for another drive and circle on the stockade, this time with their rifles leveled and ready for use. On this charge, the withering fire of the buffalo hunters was returned by a vaster, but far less deadly fire from the charging whirlwinds on horseback. The Comanches scooped up their lame and dying, carrying them out of gunshot range.

Regrouping near the creek, Quanah took command. Horse Back yielded to him because he recognized the great war cloud sitting on Quanah's brow. Horse Back sensed that his day was done, and that Quanah must now finish what he had begun. Quanah shouted out how few hunters he believed were behind the stockade, and exhorted the braves to climb over the walls on this charge, whereby they could make quick work of the buffalo hunters. The Comanche dead were already numerous; Quanah wanted to end the battle as quickly as he could.

The buffalo hunters caught their breath. The few short cheers at driving off the Comanche charge were broken up by Tilghman's shouts to reload their rifles and prepare for the next charge, which would come at any moment. No sooner had he spoken than the lookouts yelled, "Here they come again!" Their elation gave way to fear that charged the adrenalin and drove their fingers, surprisingly agile now, as they shoved cartridge after cartridge into the repeaters.

Masterson called down a different order of fire this time. "Okay men, open up anytime you're ready with the Sharps, and aim for the horses. This time we don't want them to get close."

The big buffalo guns boomed out and Comanche horses fell. But twenty or thirty horses out of six or seven hundred is a pittance, a gap that closed as quickly as it formed. The Comanches rode on, grimly determined to slay their foe. Their shouts and war cries filled the air like innumerable flocks of wild geese. As he rode, Horse Back sang his death song. He would give all he had, his life, in this charge. Happy is the man who gives up his life in this manner!

The Comanche tide neared the seemingly frail stockade walls now, nowhere higher than nine or ten feet. This time they did not split, but rode straight for the walls, where the deadly hail of bullets from the repeating rifles slashed and tore at their lines like wolves' teeth.

Quanah heard death songs all around him. He grabbed one hunter's rifle and yanked it through the crack between the poles, carrying a good chunk of flesh from the hunter's hand. As he looked up, he saw Horse Back and a half dozen other warriors on the stockade wall. All were felled like trees by the mighty saws of the Colt pistols that filled the white men's hands. Only Horse Back, whose powerful leaping charge had greater momentum, fell forward into the compound.

There was death at the walls. Quanah and the other remaining chiefs waved the tide on around the stockade and beyond, where they regrouped for another charge. This time, Quanah directed them in a fast rideby on one side of the walls, firing from under the necks of their ponies. Quanah himself peeled off the other way and concealed himself on the side of his horse as he circled by the corner where Horse Back had fallen.

The buffalo hunters were all at the side where the red wave was washing by; none saw Quanah as he slipped off his horse and threw himself over the stockade wall. Somehow, in the general fear, Amos had stayed calm. He sensed Quanah behind him and whirled. Betraying his own kind, he yelled out, "Comanche!" He did not fire, but three others quickly did. Quanah had Horse Back on his shoulder and had just leaped for the top of the wall; his right hand caught. A bullet tore through his right side, smashing his lower ribs. He tumbled to the ground; gathering his legs under him, he immediately leaped again. Another slug ripped through his thigh, causing him to falter at the top, a perfect target for all the guns aimed at him. From all the trials of his short life, he gathered his strength and pulled high—one foot now on the wall, moving slightly quicker than those trying to kill him. As he leapt free, one more bullet caught him high on the shoulder and drove him over the wall. He grabbed the mane of his horse with his one good hand and half ran, half rode with Horse Back on his shoulder down to the trees along the creek.

Most of the Comanches and Kiowas had witnessed Quanah's bravery at saving Horse Back from mutilation by the enemy. Now he could be buried and enter the next world as a whole spirit, the heart of the Comanche way.

Inside the compound, voices rattled on as to why they couldn't stop the Comanche who had dropped among them like a swift eagle.

Amos spoke sharply, "That was Quanah, Dixon. I know it was Quanah."

Masterson chimed in, "Whoever it was, we filled him full of lead, and he just kept going. Tilghman, did you ever see anything like that?"

"Nope. That was Quanah, alright. None of the other Comanches quite have his size or face. I was sure we got him, though. I know he was hit at least three or four times."

"Hah!" Jackman roared. "You could hit Quanah ten times and still not kill him when his medicine is that strong. Quanah was eagle today. We think we shoot him, but just hit feathers!" And another snort of derision at the white hunters burst from Amos, out of the depth of his Comanche blood.

Quanah was indeed badly wounded as he lay in the shade of the tall cottonwoods, but the wounds were clean. Red Horse stanched the bleeding with willow leaves and an herb balm. Quanah was still very much in charge. He knew now their early tactics had taken an incredible toll. Close to a third of their number were dead, disabled by their wounds, or horseless.

He now dispersed a band of Kiowa Apaches to the far side of the stockade to draw the fire of the buffalo hunters. Keeping the main force in reserve, he sent lone riders racing toward the stockade gate to try to tear it down.

The buffalo men were not fooled by the ploy, but stayed scattered around the walls. As they saw the lone rider heading for the gate, they divined his mission. He kept coming through a hail of bullets that cut swaths through the tall prairie grasses. None of the buffalo hunters had ever seen the likes of what unfolded under their eyes.

The Comanche stayed on his horse to the end and rode it full gallop headlong into the gate, breaking the horse's neck. The scream of the dying horse stabbed the open sky, ripping it apart. The rider and horse went down in a heap, and a blanket of lead buried them there. The crossbar was split and almost broken by the violent impact. Only the wagons behind the gate held it.

Again Masterson spoke, seeing the need. "Grab that wagon tongue. We'll have to make it do. This crossbar won't take much more pounding."

The crossbar was wedged on top of the wagon tongue, making it stronger and tighter. More weight, bales of old hides, were stacked both in the wagon and beneath it to absorb the blows.

The next rider never made the gate, thanks to Billy Dixon's sharpshooting. The third and fourth riders did. Again, the screams of the dying horses shrieked in the ears of those who listened. The fourth rider managed to scramble away, and, carrying several bullet wounds, crawled back to where the Comanches could pick him up on horseback. He reported to Quanah before he died on how stout the gate seemed to be. Quanah sent no more riders.

The battle settled down now to a siege. On all sides, the Comanches would ride within rifle range, exchange a few shots and withdraw. Their ammunition was running low, but not the buffalo hunters'.

On a high butte across the creek, at least a mile from Adobe Walls, three Indians sat on their horses watching the battle. One was Ishtai, naked but for a breechclout, painted blue from toe to hair. The other two were Kiowa and Cheyenne medicine men. Ishtai's heart was heavy within him. The Comanche dead were numerous. He knew if they had followed Quanah's plan they would have fared better attacking the bluecoats in the thick brush of the Brazos bottoms.

In the shelter of the cottonwoods, Quanah continued to direct the battle. His wounds were painful but not serious enough to cloud his mind, even with the loss of blood; he pushed the pain to the back of his head. He remembered now when Horse Back told him of the battle here against the famed Carson and the bluecoats. Though Carson had lost many men, many Quohadi died, too. There was something about this place that favored the spirit of the white man, which is why they built Adobe Walls on the grassy knoll, where they could see in all directions. Quanah knew the white man had a lot of fighting in his blood; many of them were not afraid to fight. So he persisted in trying to wear them down until nightfall, when the Comanches might close in a closer knot with this foe.

As the day wore on, the battle lessened. Several among the buffalo hunters were wounded or nicked, none seriously. Now, they gathered the Comanche spears and laid them in a pile—real trophies of war if they lived to tell about it. None, at this moment, was sure if any of them would.

Billy Dixon squinted at the faraway butte, now focused clearly with the afternoon sun at his back. Suddenly he snapped, "Amos, bring me that Sharps." Amos did as he was told.

"Now, Amos, stand right here in front of me, just like that. See that Comanche up there all painted up. I'm gonna pick him off."

Amos laughed. "Humph. You sure something, Dixon. You shoot buffalo long way off. I see you do that. This Comanche too far away, too high. Can Dixon shoot eagle from the sky?"

"Hell, I plugged that Quanah. For all I know he may be breathing his last. I'm gonna get this one, too."

"Quanah run too fast for dying man. Maybe you have better luck here."

"Thanks, Amos, for wishing me luck. Now if you'll just stand still."

Amos stood straight as a pole. Dixon raised the sights for the distance, which looked to be about a mile. Then he steadied his aim.

They had the attention of nearly all the men. The hunters watched attentively. As Dixon's finger tightened, some of them felt their own trigger fingers twitch in response. The bullet that sped aloft was a winged messenger, with all the hopes of the desperate frontiersmen speeding it on.

As the loud crack of the rifle boomed away, Dixon swore aloud, "I missed! The sucker missed!"

"Nope, the sucker hit." Masterson corrected him. "Not the painted Comanche, the one next to him."

All eyes strained to witness the drama unfolding on the butte that reared its head in the east. Ishtai left it to the Cheyenne to gather up the Kiowa who had been sitting beside him; he knew his medicine was broken. Great shame filled him as he rode up before

Quanah to tell him his medicine was gone. Quanah looked at Ishtai, his old childhood friend, in silent disgust for a full moment. Then, abruptly, he gave the order to withdraw. The Comanche had a long ride to make and many dead to bury in the ancestral Palo Duro Canyon.

The buffalo hunters watched the Comanche and Kiowa go with whoops and shouts of joy. "Dixon, you did it!"

"Billy Dixon, God bless those pea-picking eyes of yours. You picked that Indian clean off his horse."

They spent a sleepless night, standing guard and waiting for the Comanches to return. The next morning, with the prairie swept as empty as the sky, they packed up to return to Santa Fe. There would be no buffalo hunting that season, not when the Comanches were out in such force. For the rangy buffalo hunters, the battle of Adobe Walls was over.

CHAPTER XXVIII ISHTAI'S LAST MEDICINE

When the Comanches camped that night with their allies, the Kiowas, there was no singing. All knew the defeat they had suffered. Horse Back, their great chief, was dead; Quanah now took his place. None questioned Quanah's authority. He, alone, leaped into the pit of the hunters and returned alive, bearing Horse Back on his shoulder. His three wounds slowed him terribly in mounting his horse, but once mounted, he could still ride.

The Comanches lost their great war chief, but their loss was ameliorated by the presence of Quanah. Quanah stood larger in their eyes now; he had counseled against this raid. The Kiowas had lost their chief medicine man, and now they wanted revenge.

Around the campfire, Kicking Bird mixed a dish of poisoned meat. All had seen him and knew what it contained. Now he passed the dish to Quanah; only Quanah could determine what must be done.

Quanah said nothing, but thought a long moment, then rose, stepped across the campfire, and handed it to Ishtai, who was watching his every move.

"Eat!" was the sole word Quanah uttered, then returned to his place, where he sat stoically, unmindful of his wounds, and watched Ishtai eat the poisoned meat.

ISHTAI'S LAST MEDICINE

Ishtai had little desire to eat. But it was easier than looking upward and telling Quanah no. It was only a short while after he swallowed the meat before he felt the poison grip his bowels. He leapt to his feet and ran into the darkness, where, with his spirit fast running like water into sand, he let out a terrible moan and died, his medicine broken.

The faces of the Kiowas carried a grim satisfaction, as did some of the Comanches. Quanah pitched a few more buffalo chips on the fire. His face betrayed no emotion. He could take no satisfaction in seeing his old friend Ishtai die, though it was the Comanche way. His eyes glowed like stars in the deep night sky. No one gazed at them for long.

At the Comanche camp, there was much weeping and wailing as the women counted their dead. Horse Back's death was the hardest to bear. His head was gray, for he had seen many days. His lips had told many stories of the greatness of the Comanches in the past. His eyes had witnessed many of those great deeds, his hands performed them. Truly one of the fathers and grandfathers had passed away.

Tonarcy took some comfort in the heroic action of her Quanah. But she, too, filled with dread and foreboding at thought of the days that lay ahead. With Horse Back's death, some of the glory and brightness of the old days were gone. She asked Quanah, "Where will all the women, who have no man, sleep now, Quanah? Who will feed their children?"

Quanah spoke slowly, and with unaccustomed gravity to Tonarcy. "I must fulfill the old pattern for the Quohadi. I will take four of the women in my tent. You go and pick the four, Tonarcy. Pick the young ones who can bear many warriors. Pick those you know who do not have quarreling tongues, who will obey you as well as me. Also, pick those you know will please Quanah. Pick widows whose children will be good ones. The other warriors will follow Quanah."

The Comanche camp was restless. The raids and war parties were more numerous. Quanah was no longer content to merely take the ranchers' horses and cows. Where possible now, he shed their blood, or took their wives before killing them, much as the youngest braves did. He knew there was a madness in his veins that must burn itself out.

Only Tonarcy among his wives could quiet the thunder in his blood. The others could slake his lust; only she could slake his sorrow. He often remembered the beauty of his mother. Now Tonarcy nurtured him and received his love and pent-up emotions in return. She was both mother and wife to this wild eagle who led the Comanche. Her heart beat fiercely within her as she pondered what she meant to Quanah. She was gentle with his other wives, even Mala, the Mescalero, who was with child, and told them to do only what they would have done on their own accord.

CHAPTER XXIX   BUFFALO WALLOW

At Santa Fe only a few days passed before several of the buffalo hunters grew restless. "What's out there? What's happening?" ran the questions.

Tilghman, Dixon, Jackman, Philips, Brewster, and Burns decided to ride to Fort Sill and give a personal report on Adobe Walls to the army. Unless the army drove the Comanches onto the reservation, there would be no room on the plains for white buffalo hunters, ever.

Tilghman especially thought it would be worth a try. They put together their grubstake, and signed on as army scouts to draw their first pay. Then, with five extra horses carrying their goods, they set out across the staked plains. The sun was warming the air now, though winter was not quite through.

As luck would have it, they swung too far north of Adobe Walls. As they headed south again, they ran into a war party of over a hundred Comanches, most of whom had been at Adobe Walls, led by Ten Bears.

They saw the Comanches about three miles off, shortly after the Comanches had seen them. Tilghman, thinking fast, said, "Boys, head for that buffalo wallow over there. That's the only cover we will find out here."

The six men rode as they had never ridden before. Here there were no stockade and adobe walls to protect them. Only a buffalo wallow, maybe four feet deep and twenty yards across. With a little coaxing, they were able to lay their horses down, though they knew they wouldn't stay down when the shooting started. The Comanches rode low; they would make a close pass.

The wave of horses broke and flowed around the wallow. Bullets poured in and out of the rounded bowl of earth. A few Comanches went down. One recognized Jackman and yelled, "We get you, Amos!"

Two of the hunters' horses were dead, two more lay wounded and dying. Tilghman knew they must save their other horses to save their skins. He ordered Amos and Burns to lay down in the middle of the wallow and hold the horses. With herculean effort, they dragged the dead horses to the rim of the wallow in the direction of the Comanches. Now, with some breastworks, they could open up sooner with their repeaters.

The charge was not long in coming. This time their fire was more deadly, and they drove the Comanches off quickly. The Comanches pulled back about a mile and waited awhile, planning their strategy.

Dixon lay down his rifle, too hot to touch, and reloaded his other Winchester. "Ben, they're gonna get us. We'll get a lot more of them. But all they got to do is wait until dark. Then they'll shorten our hair."

"Maybe so, Billy, maybe not. It appears it's getting dark before the sun goes down. Lookee there!" They all looked to the north where his hand stretched out.

A blue norther reached across the sky and seemed to be racing itself. The cloud bank rose high, like a wall of ice and water climbing the heavens. Soon, it would shut out the sky. The Comanches saw it, too, and bailed out of the battle, beating a path eastward toward the breaks and shelter of the caprock. Tears and cries of joy exploded at the sight of the Comanches running before the storm.

"Hold on boys. We're not out of this yet. Saddle up and be ready to ride. As soon as that norther hits and gives us cover, we will ride out, too."

When a late norther hits on the high plains, the temperature can drop fifty degrees in a couple hours. This one was no exception. With the forty-mile wind at their backs, the plainsmen flew like winged deer.

By late evening, they were off the caprock and in a small canyon. They gathered dry cedar limbs and built a roaring fire beneath an overhang to warm themselves and their horses. Dixon swore he was so cold he could crawl right into the fire.

Three days later they rode into Fort Sill, still shaken by the close call they had with the Comanches. Adobe Walls was miracle enough; another hand of God, like the blue raging blizzard that drove off the Comanches, was almost too much—like lightning striking twice in the same spot.

Nelson Miles, the commander at Fort Sill, received them graciously in his own quarters. His pretty yellow-haired wife, Sarah, brought them coffee and slices of cake she had just baked.

Amos, the Indian, hunkered down in a corner and said nothing, but ate his cake and gulped his hot coffee gladly. Dixon and Tilghman did the talking.

"Colonel, this same storm that just died down saved our lives up there on the high plains. We were riding from Santa Fe to tell you about Adobe Walls . . ."

"Adobe Walls! What happened there? We heard there had been a big battle, but nothing further. Were you there?"

"Were we? I'll say! But I'll let Dixon tell you that story. Anyway, the Comanche are out in force, greater war parties than I've ever heard tell of. A band of maybe two hundred caught up to us and pinned us down all day in a buffalo wallow. They would have eventually lifted our scalps but for that blue norther that dropped down on us like tar from a bucket. It gave us the cover we needed to escape. We killed a bunch of them as they made several passes; they killed half of our mounts."

"God be thanked, boys. You're lucky to be here. Now what took place at Adobe Walls? I'll swear you boys have seen some sights these past few days."

Dixon now spoke up. "Yes, sir, we've seen some sights, and it's a wonder our hair ain't gray or missing. There were twenty-eight of us, including one woman, holed up at the Walls waiting for a break in the weather. One night the crossbeam on the roof busted and woke us all up." Tilghman was glad Dixon politely refrained from mentioning his gunshot into the roof.

"Well, we stayed up the rest of the night. At first light, the Sadler brothers went down to the creek in a wagon to get some fresh cottonwood timbers. They saw the Comanche first and luckily got off the one shot that alerted us.

"Colonel, I hope you can understand what I am about to say. There was a thousand or more Comanches, Kiowas, and southern Cheyenne bearing down on us out of the north in full headdress and battle cry. With their lances, they rode over the Sadlers like they was match sticks. They was four or five deep in horses, breast to breast, and stretched out to near half a mile. Like I say, Colonel, I hope you understand me, cause till my dying day, that's the prettiest sight I could hope to see. It were terrible but pretty. Do you get me, Colonel?"

"Yes, Dixon, I know what you mean exactly. I was at Gettysburg and saw Pickett's charge. I had the same feeling then, a feeling that I would never come out of it alive, but that I was glad to see the beauty of that charge. Go on."

"Well, luckily some wasn't as dazzled as I was. Tilghman here was checking out the rifles and ammunition, the military issue. Them new repeaters saved us. Bat Masterson wheeled two heavy wagons behind the stockade gate, that saved us, too.

"Masterson had us hold our fire till they were right up on us, so the element of surprise was with us. Then we opened up on them, and we must have slew fifty or a hundred of them right there. They looked like they would ride their horses right over the stockade. We shot several off the wall including one of their big chiefs. Amos thinks it was Horse Back. Anyway, they regrouped and made another charge, this time just riding by and firing from under the necks of their horses. We was letting them have it again, when several of us heard a rustling of feathers behind us."

Miles leaned forward intently as Dixon, gripped by the same passion with which he had fought, told his story.

"Well, we whirled and there was another big chief, a young one with eagle feathers reaching to his knees. Amos thinks it was Quanah Parker . . ."

Amos spoke for the first time. "It was Quanah, okay. I tell you that."

"Well, all of us shot at this Quanah, and several hit him. He had to be hit three or four, maybe five times. Once he slipped, but finally he gathered that old chief on his shoulder and carried him up right over that wall.

"We stood them off like that all day. By afternoon, they was trying something new. They'd send a buck at a time, riding low on a fast horse, and kill the dang horse, breaking his neck at full gallop running it into the gate. Luckily those wagons and the hides we piled behind the gate held."

Dixon was a bit shy about telling of his own heroic role, and hesitated now. Ben Tilghman noticed, and picked up the thread of the story.

"We would have still been there, Colonel, if it hadn't been for Dixon! There was a butte sticking up about three hundred feet into the air, a mile off to the east across the creek. In late afternoon you could see those three Injuns plain as day sitting on their horses and watching the battle. One was buck naked and painted blue, or maybe black.

"Dixon called up Amos here, balanced his long bore Sharps buffalo gun on his shoulder, and adjusted the sights for distance. Well, Dixon's buffalo hunting the year before stood him in good stead. He guessed the distance just right, but didn't allow for windage. He knocked one of them Injuns right off his horse, not the medicine chief he aimed at, but it don't matter which one. It was a hell of a shot.

"The Comanches were broken up by this. They took it to be powerful bad medicine, and in light of the drubbing they had taken all day, it gave them a good reason to clear out. We couldn't believe it until the next day, but that prairie was as clean as a wolf's tooth.

"So we lit out for Santa Fe, and as soon as we got outfitted, we rode back here and got trapped in that buffalo wallow for another day or we'd have been here sooner."

Miles was stunned by the wealth of the stories, but recognized their import. "Are you men sworn in as regular army scouts?"

"I was sworn in at Santa Fe so I could draw enough pay to get supplies and head here, but none of these others have signed papers."

"It doesn't matter. You were regular army from Santa Fe on, as far as I am concerned. I am recommending you all for the Congressional Medal of Honor. The country will be electrified by this news and we'll put an end to the Indian problem once and for all."

Bill Philips had to work at hiding his disgust. He had never cared for Yankees, and as a matter of fact liked most Indians, particularly the Shoshones and Flatheads, more than he liked Yankees. He knew he would get this medal not because of his bravery, and he had been brave enough, but because of the army's need for publicity. The hypocrisy of it filled his craw.

Tilghman noted Philips' mood and knew he shared some of it. "Well, thank you, Colonel. We did our duty, and fought just to save our scalps. Right now, we could stand a good long sleep in a warm bed. If you want to give us a medal, well, that's okay."

"Sergeant, show these men to their quarters, and double up on the blankets. Tilghman, you stay here. I wish to talk to you further."

When the others had gone, Miles opened up again about the medals. "You see, Tilghman, ours is a Christian nation. There's probably more preachers back east than we have soldiers in the army. When the jury down in Jacksboro sentenced the two Kiowa chiefs to death, you should have seen the uproar in the Boston papers. You know what kind of murdering rascals Satanta and Big Tree were. Well, these eastern preachers, and I respect them for their convictions, feel the redskin is a child and not responsible for his deeds. They think the good book is the only way to civilize the savage, and perhaps in the long run they're right. Of course they've never faced a war party like the two you have just seen. If I get the Medal of Honor for six army scouts, and Sherman will back me up with President Grant, then that's a different matter. We will get the extra troops to corral the Comanche in his den and stop him. The sword will put this Quanah on the reservation, and then the Quakers with the holy Word can make a Christian out of him."

"Well, Colonel, I see what you mean. In a way my heart is with Dixon and Philips and Jackman. The plains won't be the same when the Comanches are pushed onto the reservation. But I don't think I want to see a war party that size again. Once was enough, twice too much. I'll talk to the boys. You can give us those medals."

CHAPTER XXX   FORT SILL

Mackenzie was elated when he heard the news about Adobe Walls and the buffalo wallow fight. "Do you know what this means, Calhoun? The Comanches are finished. No more sniping. This is war. Now, you'll see some action."

Calhoun remembered these words with foreboding as he accompanied Mackenzie to Fort Sill, where General William Tecumseh Sherman gathered all the area commandants from Fort Union, Fort Dodge, Fort Smith, Fort Griffin, Fort Richardson, and Fort Concho.

There, they were briefed on the two battles by a tall, lean buffalo hunter, Ben Tilghman, who had been in both fights. The stories were mighty impressive. Calhoun knew the Comanches had raised that large a force only two or three times before: when they drove the Apaches out of the central hills; when they drove the Spanish out of San Saba; and after the courthouse fight in San Antonio, when San Antonio was perhaps the only settlement spared destruction. With Quanah as war chief, that force would stay together.

Sherman's eyes glittered like fresh dew in sunlight. "We will have all the troops and supplies we need. President Grant has given me a free hand. The Comanche, Kiowa, and other southern plains tribes are to be forced onto the reservations, disarmed, and dismounted. Any resistance will be crushed. Are there any proposed battle plans?"

Mackenzie rose with a "Yes, sir!" and walked proudly and stiffly to the large area map showing the rivers draining off the limestone caprock of the high plains. Tilghman studied him carefully. Here was their wolf, he thought. The handsome sideburns and moustache, brown to auburn, were a mask for the cold steel inside this man. The unblinking eyes and forceful direct manner unfolded a firm, almost fanatical desire to be at the point in the last campaign to crush the Comanches.

Mackenzie held the audience in thrall as he outlined what was known of the Comanche habits. Calhoun taught him well, and Calhoun often heard his own words and phrases pouring from Mackenzie's mouth. "We know the Comanches are great horsemen. The Comanche warrior always keeps a string of five to six horses. Two hundred warriors means a herd at their base camp of over a thousand horses.

"From Tilghman's description, then, Horse Back and Quanah must have gathered all the existing tribes left for their blow on Adobe Walls. Since the War of Rebellion and the removal of the Clear Fork reservation to Fort Sill, we have never found the Comanche camped in small bands the way they were before the war.

"We do know they have a special winter quarters they retreat to. They strike and melt back into the earth like serpents. All other tribes call them serpents in their sign language." Mackenzie drew his hand wriggling backward through the air, and Calhoun had the flashing thought that Mackenzie had changed; given enough time, Mackenzie would, even with his hatred, become part Comanche, too.

Ranald Mackenzie had prepared for this moment, and now he pressed his points home. "My Tonkawa scouts, after having, uh, talked to some Comanche squaws we captured, tell me there's a deep canyon somewhere in here, where the Comanches hole up for the winter.

"We know it's not on the Brazos. The Double Mountain fork is the longest, and there's no canyon there. I've been up the Salt Fork myself. The Canadian was a likely bet, but the buffalo hunters in recent years have explored the Canadian and no canyon as huge as the Tonkawas describe has been found.

"The Arkansas has been explored. That leaves the Red River, which has three forks, maybe more. I'll put my bet on this center fork here. The beaver trappers who first drew this map trapped many beaver on this stream; it runs a lot of water. Here is the largest canyon. The Mexicans at Santa Fe know about it, too. A few of them have been there to trade rifles with the Comanches. They call it the Palo Duro.

"My plan is this: five full companies converge from these five forts, leaving on such a schedule so as to arrive there about the same time. A full brigade from Fort Smith and Fort Sill should follow with enough supplies for a month-long campaign and mopping-up operation. The Comanches will be moving this summer. We will try to hold their depredations to a minimum, but not invade their territory directly. Then, when they are in their winter den in late October, we will strike!"

Sherman was obviously pleased with the plans. "Excellent. I believe Mackenzie has developed adequate intelligence for us to go on. It will take nearly this long to prepare the campaign. Double the patrols this summer. Report every sighting of the hostiles. When winter's at hand, the Red River Campaign will begin."

CHAPTER XXXI   FATHER PEYOTE

Quanah sensed that the lull in the army's actions was only a calm before the storm. The southern plains were free of buffalo hunters that summer, but the hunters farther north in Nebraska and Kansas had taken their toll. The migration of the shaggy beasts came only in trickles. The Quohadi turned increasingly to other game.

Other clans, the Penatekas, the Coth-cho-tekas, drifted steadily onto the reservation at Fort Sill. Only the Quohadis, the antelope clan, stayed completely together under Quanah. Many of the young warriors from the other clans joined the Quohadi rather than be at the mercy of the white man's handout.

Quanah knew his medicine must be strong in the months ahead. Father Peyote was properly seasoned now. By ones and twos, then in small groups, Quanah initiated his tribe into its use. He taught them the rituals of purification, of meditation, that they might be in the proper frame of mind when they chewed on the mysterious cactus buds and entered the spirit world. He showed them the figures in that spirit world were brighter, more colorful images of the things in this world; how, when their minds were prepared, the Great Spirit of all things would come and reveal himself to them in a rainbow cloud of flashing lights, a vision of his true totem, the wolf; and how the vision following this one would be the one they would need to know, the one wherein the Great Spirit unfolded the future to them as in their namedreams.

Many young warriors had difficulty in having a namedream now through meditation. Quanah taught them the use of Father Peyote to take with them on their namedream vigil. He showed them how Father Peyote must not be abused and relied on by himself, but used in connection with the traditional Comanche practices of tobacco, cedar incense, and proper meditation, the emptying of one's self before the Great Spirit.

Thus Quanah became medicine chief for the Comanches as well as war chief for the bands still gathered into his tribe. Their spirit was indeed strong. The old ways of the Comanche returned in strength. Even the scarcity of the buffalo led them into new resourcefulness in finding game. But as numerous as Quanah's tribe now became, the numbers were few in comparison to those gathering against him.

The remaining Kiowas were restless. They had lost their medicine chief at Adobe Walls, and none had come to take his place. They traveled far to partake in a sun dance with the Cheyenne and Sioux to gather strength. The news of Quanah's medicine and its magic reached them in late summer.

Quanah sent his most trusted men to seek out the Kiowa in the Anadarko hills and the remnants of the southern Cheyenne along the Arkansas to come and winter in the Palo Duro Canyon where the deer were plentiful, where there was always grass for their horses.

As the summer ended and the chill blasts of autumn began to flay the leaves from the trees, the various bands gathered, clambering gingerly down the few steep trails into the vast Palo Duro Canyon, the stronghold of the Comanches.

CHAPTER XXXII TWO DIFFERENT PATHS

Mackenzie left Fort Griffin with a platoon for a final strategy session at Fort Sill. He would rendezvous later with his full company at the Medicine Mounds near the Pease River.

Miles and Sherman were glad to see Mackenzie. His confidence led them to believe they were not on a wild goose chase, but at last might engage the Comanches in force, and cripple their warfare capability in one blow. They knew many eyes, not least those of President Grant, were upon them. Their chance for additional glory and honor was at hand.

Mackenzie assured them that his Tonkawa scouts had made additional inquiries among all the Texas Indians during the summer, especially the peaceful Wacos and Caddos who often traded with the Comanches. The existence of the great canyon was no longer in doubt. It explained how the Comanches could seemingly melt back into the ground after their raids. With the location pinpointed to one of the forks of the Red River, Mackenzie had no doubt they would find it. The key was the coordination of the companies to allow them to converge on the canyon together. Mackenzie pointed out that, as his men went up on the caprock that began the staked plains here at the White River, a fork of the Brazos, he would send out scouts to link up with the companies from Fort Dodge and

Fort Union. They would slow their advance in hopes of triangulating the attack.

With the three companies hitting first from the north, south, and west, they hoped to drive the Comanches east, where the mop-up brigades from Fort Smith and Fort Sill would capture whoever they didn't kill.

Sherman was extremely pleased with the plan. He intended to recommend Mackenzie for a general's star if it went well. The last night before departure there was a rollicking square dance with five fiddlers in the mess hall at Fort Sill. The same night, many miles away in the deep canyon beneath the western sea of stars, Quanah was leading the first large group peyote ceremony of all his warriors.

In a great tepee built for the occasion, with a wide hole at the top, Quanah led the chiefs in first, singing their traditional chants. They entered from the north, as the Comanche many long years before had entered the great plains from the north. They circled counter-clockwise to the west, swung south, then east, then to the center. As over two hundred warriors entered in single file behind the chiefs, in slow rhythmic step and chant, Quanah drew the concentric circles tighter around the mysteries in the center.

Some of the Comanches carried their water drums, brass bowls bartered from the Comancheros, half filled with water and covered with antelope skins tightened by lead shot. These water drums began to speak now, and the tent became a drum, speaking with bass tones deeply tuned to the land beneath; the Palo Duro itself responded, speaking with a throbbing resonance to the Comanches.

In the middle of the tent, Quanah heaped ashes from other peyote fires, shaping a great eagle. To the north of the eagle was formed a moon. To the south, a sun sitting in the ears of a wolf. Beneath the eagle's feet was a fresh fire. Heaps of white ash in the firelight showed the eagle to be lifting its wings out of the fire. To the eye of God, looking through the opening to the heavens, the sun, the moon, the wolf, and the eagle were all illuminated. The human voices and the drum beats rose up like a mighty wind.

As the Comanches spread their peyote blankets, they smoked tobacco as it passed. Quanah lay fresh green cedar boughs on the fire; the sharp cedar incense struck every nose. Now the women came, bearing bowls of water for their men. The peyote burned hot and dry in the men's mouths. The women left as quietly as they came, their hearts full as they heard the songs roll up toward the heavens.

The fiddles struck up old Scottish and Irish folk tunes, hundreds of years old. These Scotch-Irish had been going to war to this music for a long time. The more military tunes drew forth some heavy jigs. The lyrical love melodies brought out the reels. *Soldier's Joy* was a favorite; then *To A Wild Rose.* Mackenzie chose this one to ask Sarah Miles to dance. She wore a yellow brocade dress with full skirts that matched the color of her hair. In the lamplight, she was a vision of beauty, beauty that could lead one to doom, or lead safely through one's doom and home again.

Mackenzie was in a gay, lighthearted mood. In his own mind, he had already defeated the Comanches many times over. He had not been this happy since before the Civil War, when he squired the officers' daughters at the West Point graduation ball.

He was feeling his oats and laughingly said, "If I had you to come home to, I know I'd return from this campaign."

Sarah blushed slightly. "You will return. I am sure of it. My prayers will go with you."

"Only your prayers?"

She blushed again. "No, my hopes, too. You have my hand now. What more do you want?"

"If it were not already given, I would ask your heart." And he pressed her close as he swept her across the floor, his elegant limp hardly evident.

Father Peyote chewed in the mouths of the Comanches. The door in the roof of their heads opened and they followed Quanah into the spirit world. He told many ancient stories of the Comanche ancestors, how they left their home with the Shoshone on the Snake River far beyond the mountains, the coming of the Spaniards with the horse, the god-dog the Comanche mastered and made their own. He spoke of the old feud with the Kiowas, and how, under the wise counsel of Green Buffalo, the Comanches and the Kiowas smoked the peace pipe, and ever after rode together as equals. He spoke of the distant kin of the Numernah, the Nahuatl, the pyramid builders of Mexico, and how they, too, painted the eagle clutching the serpent as one of their holy signs; how even though the races had been sundered long before by the Great Spirit, many of their words remained the same like the name of Father Coyote.

The fiddles were in full voice now. As they broke into *Turkey in the Straw,* the din of the singing and dancing nearly raised the roof. Many a jug of whisky was being nipped at, against regulations, outside the hall; the men would return, rosy cheeked, and rejoin the dancing.

Miles took his wife in arm to dance to the strains of *Lorena,* the favorite of the Confederates during the war. "My dear, you cut quite a figure with young Mackenzie. What do you think of him?"

"Well, he's very gallant and dashing. All the more so, since he seems to be so doomed in this Indian war. He is the type a young girl might give her heart to for one night, but not forever."

It was just the answer Miles wished to hear, which made him suspect it slightly. "His will be the glory of the campaign if it succeeds. I've just arranged with General Sherman for him to replace me here at Fort Sill and nursemaid the reservation. My next assignment will be in a field command against the Sioux in the Dakotas. There, the chance for my general's star will surely come."

"Where will that leave me, dear?"

"I don't think I want you back east with your family. Perhaps St. Louis. We will take a house."

"That will be wonderful!" And she smiled radiantly. Miles thought that even though he had been married to this beauty for ten years now, he hardly knew her.

With the announcement of the next dance, Mackenzie was at her elbow again asking for the honor. She gladly assented, despite the glowering looks she received from Nelson. A little jealousy always added spice to a man's ardor.

The vision was full and commanding now. Not every Comanche saw it, but they heard those speak who saw it, and so they, too, believed. The vision grew more radiant and blissful. Quanah's voice carried like an arrow, bore them up on his eagle's wings. Their voices rang as one together, their spirits joined and lifted higher, still higher, till they joined with the voices of the upper air. . . .

CHAPTER XXXIII　　　　　　PALO DURO CANYON

Quanah rose early, while his whole family lay sleeping. He would ride up the canyon this morning and bring back a deer. He remembered how his father, Noconah, would rise before the first light for the morning's hunt. Now he was fulfilling the same pattern.

The old bucks were wise; when they bedded down, they were almost impossible to find. His favorite Appaloosa pony shivered and stamped while Quanah slipped a rope around its nose and neck. Under the stroking of his rough hands and the quiet, steady music of his voice, the horse grew calm. Most of the Comanche horse herd grazed further down the canyon where it widened and the grasses were yet thick and plenty.

Quanah slipped up on the horse's back and nudged with his knees. The Appaloosa quickly picked up into a trot that carried Quanah out of the sprawling Comanche camp into the woods, the thick willows and cottonwoods that thronged the clear running stream, the Prairie Dog Town Fork of the Red River.

He knew he would find a buck drinking at the river's edge after browsing all night. The breath from the pony's and Quanah's noses steamed in the bitter early-morning light. It was cold, but Quanah barely felt it on his bare arms and back. He wore only leggings. Long ago he had learned one was more alert when staying slightly cold. He had to be alert to see the deer.

There they were, two yearling does across the stream. Quanah nudged his pony on. The buck would be near. Quanah had brought only his bow, and he wished to shoot it but once. This was the way to hunt the deer.

Then he saw it, the antlers spreading as wide as his own wide shoulders. The arrow was already nocked in the string. He slowed the pony to the slowest walk possible. The handsome buck, twice the size of the does, may have heard the pony's unshod hoof strike a stone. Whatever the reason, he ceased drinking and slowly turned away from the stream. As he came out of the willows he was in full view, and Quanah drew the bowstring tight. The buck saw Quanah and sensed his peril, but in that imperceptible pause before flight, the arrow flew. Quanah prayed steadily to the Great Spirit of the hunt; his aim and mark were true. The buck leaped upward, as if to gain the canyon rim in one bound. Then he fell, his lifeblood seeping from his wound.

Quanah jumped to the ground and followed on foot with another arrow at the ready. But as he came upon the buck, he saw the arrow had hit home. He spoke a quiet prayer aloud to the mighty buck who yielded his life that Quanah's family might eat.

Quickly, he gutted and dressed it with his knife, cutting off the strong scent glands on the backs of the legs. The arrow had cut the major arteries near the heart. Quanah slid the arrow back out through the ribs and placed it in his quiver where it could share the deer's blood with the other arrows. He cut away the heart and ate it on the spot, savoring its tough but chewy texture and the warm blood in his mouth. The tender liver he placed in his tote sack for Tonarcy.

Then, with the deer slung across the pony in front of him, he rode back into the Comanche camp, now astir with life. As he looked down through the canyon, the early morning sun was touching the tops of the canyon walls. The light bounced off the red, yellow, and ochre clays, filling the air with its radiance. Many campfires sent their juniper and buffalo chip smoke into the air. Quanah sat silently for a moment and let his eyes and whole being grow full with the satisfaction of his hunt and the beauty of his village as it woke with the sun.

Tonarcy and Mala were already outside, stirring the campfire and carrying water to the cooking pot. Mala's new son was strapped to her back. Tonopah, Quanah's first son, was three now, and ran, naked and free, from the fire to the river's edge and back.

When they saw the big deer, Tonarcy cooed and chuckled with

joy, and Mala did a little dance, which the baby on her back seemed to like. "Quanah! Quanah! What a great deer! We shall have to share it with other families. Come, Mala, bring your knife. The fire can tend itself for a while."

Quanah tied his horse to a young cottonwood behind the tepee, and sought his tobacco for a morning smoke as he hunkered by the fire. The tobacco and cedar smoke filled his nose and put an edge on his appetite. He lay a few more sticks of dried juniper on the fire.

After breakfast, which took some time since he had to sit and listen quietly while his eight wives burned his ears with praises, he rose and went to look for his young son who was already off exploring the river.

The young Comanche boy still held his summer tan, his skin as brown as a buckeye. He had found something very unusual on the sandy canyon floor. It was a great black tarantula, as big as a man's hand. The boy knew no fear. He held his stick out to block the tarantula's path. The sudden violent motion of the tarantula struck fear into the boy's heart. The tarantula suddenly reared on his hind legs and clawed the air with his four hairy front legs.

The boy felt his father's hand on his shoulder. Quanah looked down at the small drama. "Let the hairy one go in peace, my son. All creatures have their place on earth. If we hinder them, something one day may hinder us; even the river is like this. You can only stop its flow for a while. More rain will come and one day wash out the beaver's dam, no matter how high it is."

"What does the beaver do then?"

"He swims. Then later he builds again."

They walked, Quanah's hand on his head, back toward the camp where Quanah meant to string a small bow for him with some of the deer's tendons.

As they walked, a vague foreboding began to gather in Quanah. Whenever he had felt this before, danger had been near, as on that time his mother had been captured, after that morning hunt from which his father had never returned. He looked at the canyon rims. Nothing on the north rim. On the southeast rim the sun had just climbed above the canyon wall and was hard to look into.

But the eagle can look into the sun, and Quanah did. At first he caught a swatch of bright blue, that went away. Then returned. Then more blue, a glimpse of silver as the sun glanced off an unsheathed sword.

Quanah was running now, his son scooped up under one arm. He ran all through the camp crying his warning. At his own lodge he gathered up his rifles, bows and arrows, all his weapons, instructed one wife to lead his horse up the canyon before turning it loose, and the others to gather up the deer meat already cut and head for high ground on the walls of the canyon. The whole Comanche tribe fled to the thick junipers on the sloping walls of the canyon, the junipers whose hard, durable wood gave the Comanches their bows and the canyon its Spanish name, Palo Duro.

Mackenzie's scouts had discovered the canyon the night before. Only after a morning's reconnoitering had they found the Comanche camp. Mackenzie could have waited for the next morning and had a surprise attack that would have caught the Comanche serpent asleep before it opened its eagle eyes. He could have waited until more than the other company from Fort Union was at hand, in contact with him, and ready to make the pincer movement he had outlined in his battle plan. Mackenzie could have waited for a number of reasons, not the least of which being that there were more Comanche warriors in the canyon than he had soldiers, and there were almost as many rifles. As it was, Mackenzie could not wait.

His scouts found a trail they could descend single file and attack in a cavalry charge from the south, folding the Comanche camp up like an accordion. He knew when they heard the shots, the other company from Fort Union would be there soon, descending the other side of the canyon, which looked less precipitous in places.

As he sat now on the rim, and watched his men descend, he unsheathed his sword, and pointed it at the camp. Quanah, if you're down there, this sword will find you, he thought to himself. If you're an eagle, let's see you fly out of this trap.

Calhoun rode up beside him. "Splendid, ain't it, Colonel?"

"You mean the canyon? Yes. Why, there's nothing like it for a thousand miles."

"No, Colonel, I meant the Comanche camp. How peaceful it looks. We may never see that sight again."

Mackenzie missed the irony in his voice. "No, Calhoun. You are too much the sentimentalist. There are lots of other Indians to fight. The Sioux. The Apache. There'll be another day."

"Well, let's make this day a good one."

The surprising sternness of this remark caught Mackenzie off guard. Then he realized that Calhoun was a true Indian fighter, who would put off the fight as long as he could, but then would fight with the fury of a boxed panther.

"Let's ride."

With his men safely in the canyon, Mackenzie formed the line of charge with his sword. The Comanche camp, a quarter mile ahead, seemed unusually quiet, though all the cooking fires were still sending their smoke into the air. His men were already instructed to raze the camp on their first charge. Their swords would pull the tents into the fires and the fires would do the rest. The return charge would be the killing charge. He motioned the bugler to begin. The trumpet notes rang out; two hundred soldiers surged forward as one, two hundred swords shone like one great long sword, drawn by an invisible hand of some god strange to this land, poised to cut down the Comanche camp like a stalk of wheat.

Mackenzie was caught up in the fury of the charge; memory of the cavalry battles under Sheridan in the Shenandoah came flooding back. His big bay gelding leapt out slightly in front of the charge, and his hand, in its cold sweat, tightened on the upraised sword.

As the line of men and horses swept through the Comanche camp the destruction was great. The large tepees fell beneath the swords and into the fires. But where were the Comanches?

The Comanches began to speak now from the slopes of the canyon. Every juniper bush and tree had two rifles or three. The Tonkawa scouts were a favorite target. Not one rode out alive.

The soldiers were not badly hit because of the quickness of their charge. Their consternation was great though, as they regrouped a half mile north of the camp. The peace of the camp and canyon was utterly broken. Now great fires flared as the dried buffalo hides, whipped and toughened by a thousand winds, burst into flames in the wholly innocent cookfires. The Comanche firing kept up, as a steady deadly threat hurled at the bluecoats who were now out of range. The soldiers yelled at each other and at Mackenzie. Calhoun grimly observed, "They were to be our meat. Now, it looks like we are their meat!"

One lieutenant, who had never fought before, came riding up to Mackenzie, the sweat pouring from his face. "Colonel, how do we get out of here?"

Mackenzie's calm had returned. "I got you in here. I'll get you out."

His mind was working at high speed now. Probably, the canyon was a steep box just above them. There would be no way out there. Soon the Comanche snipers would be above them. When were the Fort Union company and Miles coming from the east? Where were the Comanche horses? Then he saw it. Not only the way out of the trap, but a way to snatch victory from the jaws of defeat.

He remembered a tactic from Virginia, one that Stonewall Jackson's cavalry had used against them.

"Follow me, men, single file, and well apart. Regroup at the far end of the canyon."

Mackenzie raced the big bay into the shallow stream. He knew how the spray of water acted as a screen; there was more to shoot at and less to hit. As the cavalry raced back down the heart of the canyon in the river, the Comanche rifles barked constantly; here they dropped a horse, there a rider, but most of the company came through unscathed. Two of the downed riders, though badly wounded, were scooped up by other bluecoats.

As they rode out of rifle range and caught up to Mackenzie, many were puzzled as he kept riding and motioned them to spread out as they fanned down the valley. Then, as the canyon widened, there it was before them.

The Comanche horse herd, with only a dozen young boys guarding it. Now Mackenzie reined up and had the bugler sound a halt. The lust that glittered in Mackenzie's eyes shone in every other man's. The Comanche horse herd was theirs. The Comanche unhorsed would be an easy target for the brigades that would soon arrive from Forts Smith, Sill, and Dodge.

"Drive the horses out of the canyon, then south, then back up into the next big canyon cut into the caprock. Put plenty of miles between us and the Comanches. Pretty soon they'll be howling down here after their horses. Let's ride!"

Many of the bluecoats opened up with shouts of joy as they drove the horses in a stampede all the way out of the Palo Duro Canyon. When the walls broke down they turned south, and drove the horses a few more miles until they turned up Tule Canyon. The Comanche herd boys fled to cover.

Two of them emerged when they saw Quanah and a hundred warriors at his back running with long floating strides down the canyon, spread out and wary. The missing horses and the tracks told the story even before the boys hove to. Quanah sent twenty of the men on to track the herd, half to report back when the herd was found. The rest must salvage their goods and families and move the camp to the mouth of the Palo Duro where they would have a dozen ways to retreat. Quanah guessed that this must have been an advance group, as large as it was, and that many more bluecoats were coming.

He was glad his rifle had caught one of the Tonkawa scouts. As he returned to the camp, he unceremoniously cut the scalp from the Tonkawa's head. Perhaps Otter Belt would see that Quanah still remembered him.

Mackenzie and his men now had most of the Comanche horse herd boxed in at the head of Tule Canyon. Many of his men who were swearing at his folly two hours before, as they were trapped in Palo Duro, believed him to be a genius now. This faith in their commander, this trust, would last about an hour.

"Lieutenant, how many horses are we down?"

"About twenty or thirty, sir. And as for casualties . . ."

"Give me that later. In the report, list only Tonkawas killed, regulars either wounded or missing. Right now, cut out between sixty and a hundred head of the choicest Comanche mounts. They look well fed; you shouldn't have any trouble."

"No, sir. Yes, sir. Right away, sir!"

The bluecoats who had been doubled up were glad to see the horses being roped and led out. A few had tried to get up on the Comanche ponies until they found out how wild they were.

"Keep them together in a remuda, Lieutenant." The Texan-Spanish words ticked off Mackenzie's tongue like a native. "Now, the rest of you men fan around close in a semicircle on the rest of the horses. Stretch it wall to wall, and tighten the circle as much as you can."

"What now, Colonel?"

"Stand out ready! Check your carbines and be sure they are fully loaded."

Calhoun guessed what Mackenzie was planning to do, and something broke within him. He had never killed a healthy horse in his life, and he wouldn't begin now. He slid to the ground and walked toward Mackenzie on foot, his rifle in his hand.

"You ain't a gonna do it, Colonel. I won't let you."

Mackenzie quickly drew his Colt pistol and threw down on Calhoun. "Get back on that horse, Calhoun. We've got to kill these Comanche ponies. It's the only way!"

"No, it's not the only way and you know it. You're not ordering me to shoot these horses!" Calhoun was shouting now. "You're mad, Mackenzie! You've gone mad! You can't butcher the Comanches, so you will butcher their horses. I won't have any part in it! Go to hell, Mackenzie!"

"Sergeant, arrest that man. Shoot him if he resists."

Calhoun was aware of the rifles trained on him. He took his own rifle in both hands, raised it above his head, and broke it on his knee, snapping the whole stock and hammer off. "There's one less gun to do your dirty work!" Then strong hands were grabbing him. He shook them free, ripped his sergeant's stripes from his sleeve and flung them at Mackenzie. Then they had him and tied his arms fast with a rope, hands tied in front of him.

Mackenzie gave the order and the carbines started firing. The screams of the dying horses almost drowned out the continuous rifle fire. The horses milled and churned in their cauldron of blood and smoke and fire. There was no escape. A few in their frenzy tried to charge at the soldiers, but the dead bodies of other horses slowed them until the Winchesters cut them down.

The firing continued over an hour and burned an indelible imprint on the minds of the men pulling the triggers. Many had tears streaming down their cheeks. The horse to them was as dear as life, for on the plains their lives depended on horses. It was madness, like firing your rifle into your own feet and legs, until you cut them off.

Calhoun did not look. He listened. He heard the dying horses, and thought over and over again, Why this waste? Why this waste? He remembered how Grant had slaughtered his green troops in the Battle of the Wilderness, at Cold Harbor, and at Petersburg, and saw it now as the same kind of waste. These Yankees weren't men, they were machines. They produced only to waste. Calhoun thought that one day the plains would be littered with their waste.

Finally, the shooting died down. The soldiers rode closer to the horses now and silenced their death screams with shots to the head. Finally, all was silent. The battle of Palo Duro Canyon was over.

CHAPTER XXXIV							MACKENZIE'S PUDDING

By the time Miles and the other commanders had rendezvoused with Mackenzie, the Comanches had scattered. Nothing of any value was left in the ruined camp. Miles caught a few score women and children in small groups in the breaks up and down the caprock. It appeared most of the Comanches had headed north and made it to the thick timbers and wide valley of the Canadian River.

Mackenzie seemed very proud of his prizes, the hundred horses he had kept. None of his men were proud. They knew they had cut and run from the fight. None were proud of killing the horses.

Miles saw the strategic blow Mackenzie had dealt the Comanches. In his report he wrote, "The Comanches are afoot now, and facing winter in a hard and merciless land. By spring, they will be on the reservation." And he was right.

Still, Miles had no love for Mackenzie. He understood the soldiers' shame at not being able to drive the entire horse herd to Fort Sill. Miles had less experience than Mackenzie, however, and did not realize the Comanches would have trailed their horse herd all night, and in all likelihood, would have been able to steal most of it back.

Mackenzie's lame leg and his forty-mile trek on foot had prompted his decision. He would always believe he had done right.

Miles took great pleasure in giving Mackenzie his new orders, and in telling him what they said before he opened the sealed envelope from Sherman. Mackenzie would replace Miles as the commandant at Fort Sill and become the grocery clerk and nursemaid for the same Comanches and Kiowas he had been trying to kill for ten years. Mackenzie also had to eat the crow of Miles' new field command against the Sioux.

Sherman weighed all the reports. He, too, would have liked to have seen all the Comanche horseflesh. As a banker, he was averse to waste. Since Mackenzie acted precipitously, anyway, Sherman advised against his getting his general's star. Mackenzie was never to wear one.

CHAPTER XXXV

CANADIAN RIVER

When Quanah learned the fate of the horses, he was more grieved than he could remember. Only the grief of the loss of his parents, Noconah and Naduah, had touched him deeper. He knew now the harsh sorrows that would be their meat and drink this winter. Without their horses, they were without game. The women had been able to carry less than a week's provisions from the camp. Quanah, thanks to his hunt and to finding his Appaloosa pony safe, had more than most. He shared his meat as far as it would go. There was no way he could share his pony.

Before he scattered the tribe into small bands, Quanah told them that he would never walk the white man's road, that his bones would bleach on the prairie with the bones of the buffalo and the bones of their horses. He said he would not blame any who could not find meat for going to the white man's reservation. "Go there, if you must, to eat. You will eat only when and what the white man tells you to eat."

Most, if not all, who listened to Quanah's eloquent words vowed not to seek the white man's corn and cattle. The white winter that would soon descend changed the minds of most. By spring, as Mackenzie had predicted, nearly all the once-free Comanche people were on the reservation, counted daily like sheep.

CANADIAN RIVER

Quanah asked all the groups to come back together, when the snows had gone, in the holy hills far up the Canadian River. The Quohadi in his original band would be there, where they found the blue flints for their spears and arrows, for they all stayed with Quanah. A few of the strongest warriors and several old men, who harbored most fiercely the old free Comanche ways and saw in Quanah their only hope, also went with him along the Canadian River.

Quanah's wives, those carrying their children and those heavy with child, shouldered their burdens without complaint and followed their chief on his gray speckled pony. A single eagle feather stood in his hair and lifted with the chilling breeze.

In midwinter, Quanah and Tonarcy huddled beneath a buffalo robe with their small band in a hollow draw. Quanah spoke slowly, and his words were almost lost in the swirling snow. "I have seen the shadow of the wolf. Who has seen more? Now my spirit is caught up like a husk of grass in this great wind that blows from Canada.

"Horse Back told me this would happen. He said, 'Quanah, when one's spirit grows, it takes wings, some like an owl, some like the blackbird with the red patches on its wings, some like an eagle. The eagle is a lonely bird. It flies higher, sees farther, fights more fiercely for its nest than any other. You have this spirit of the eagle within you, and you must sieze the people of the Comanche like an eagle siezes the serpent, and lift them as a people up high to where they can see as you see. I have looked in many eyes, Quanah. None saw as far as what I see in you.'

"So spoke Horse Back when our people were many, our horses blackened the plain, and all others—even the whiteskins—bowed down before us.

"Now we are few. Our horses' bones lie beneath the snows on the prairie. My wives are faithful, my sons. These few old ones and their wives have dreamed the same dreams as I, and have seen the same visions.

"The white man's road is a hard road. I know it well. They value things more than people. That is why I have not walked it. Yes, I am talking aloud, Tonarcy, for my heart is bursting inside my chest. You have lived closest to that heart; you, alone, with the deep pity and boundless love in your eyes can still salve the wounds in my heart.

"Can I hear the Great Spirit talking in this wind? Yes, he talks above the wind. He tells me my spirit must grow greater than the eagle; it must equal the wind that blows hard against us. He tells me that if I do this, my spirit will always have a home here, that men will hear the Comanche and Quanah talking whenever they hear this wind.

"Here is the suffering Father Peyote told me would be mine. My people are beaten and eat the white man's food under the eyes and the guns of the bluecoats. I must take these old ones and you, too, Tonarcy, onto the white man's road.

"But now I am still free. The buffalo is gone, his horn is broken. While the Comanche eat the meat at Fort Sill, I eat the snow and the wind. This is my way. I will beat the winter. Then the bluecoats will know who it is they have defeated.

"Many years ago I saw the Texanos capture my mother under a cold winter wind like this one. All day and night I ran, to tell Horse Back what happened. Now I speak to my own spirit to tell it what has happened.

"The old ways are ending. But the people have not ended. Our numbers are few, but the Great Spirit bids us live. We have new ways to learn. If the white man listens, there is much we could teach him. Yes, the white man could stand to learn much of our ways.

"Now the wind grows fiercer. I hear the breath of the wolf blow on my back and neck. Here is more of my buffalo robe, Tonarcy. May it warm you, as your hands have warmed me for so many moons."

"Your words warm me, my great Quanah."

Then, as they leaned into each other, two huddled clumps under their buffalo robes, they seemed no longer two humans, but more nearly two golden eagles sitting in the eternal snow.

CHAPTER XXXVI   FORT SILL, 1875

Mackenzie sat on the porch of his headquarters at Fort Sill, his feet propped on the railing. His hat was on the floor beside him. It was comfortable duty in a way. Sarah Miles had been slow to move her belongings, even after Nelson had left for his next post. The massacre of Custer and all his men by Sitting Bull and Crazy Horse leading the Ogallala Dakotas, and Sitting Bull's subsequent flight into Canada had pulled nearly every available troop into the Dakotas. Now she was in St. Louis, and Mackenzie reflected that he would have to stop and spend some time in St. Louis when he went to Washington that summer to lobby for that general's star Sherman had denied him.

Running the post was dull, enervating. He left most of the details of requisition to his adjutant, and the process of distribution to the Quaker Indian Agent. The winter and spring had proved him right. Nearly all the Comanches and Kiowas had come in from the cold.

Only Quanah, his main quarry, yet eluded him. Quanah was still out there somewhere, maybe with twenty warriors, maybe a hundred, no more. When Mackenzie's scouts asked about Quanah, the fresh Comanche arrivals would beg ignorance. They said, "Quanah like the wind. Quanah's spirit is everywhere." But none knew or would disclose his whereabouts.

Mackenzie felt increasingly justified in killing the horses. That

145

had crippled the famed Comanches. The Comanche on foot was just another Indian. He had even relented against Calhoun and seen him cashiered out of the army rather than court-martialed. He hated to think about Calhoun; the thought, like a splinter under the thumbnail, always hurt.

He replaced Calhoun as aide-de-camp with Sergeant Grayson, a good-natured, hard-drinking Irishman, full of stories. He could usually talk and cajole Mackenzie out of his bleaker moods. Grayson spoke now. "Sure is quiet down there among the Indians, Colonel."

"Too quiet. This nursemaid duty puts rigor mortis in your seat. I'd put in for a transfer to fight the Apaches in Arizona, if I knew where that Quanah catamount was."

"He'll be here soon enough."

Mackenzie looked sharply at Grayson. "What makes you so sure?"

"All his people are here. He's their war chief and their medicine chief now that Horse Back is gone. They'll draw him down here just like the flowers draw a bumblebee. He'll come, either to make a peace, or to run enough of the young bucks off so he can put up a fight again. Either way, when he gets here and starts cooking up that peyote medicine of his, it won't be none too quiet, I bet you."

"You make it sound almost like fun."

"Well, we could use a little excitement."

"From that cloud of dust, a rider is burning a little leather and horsehide to get here. Maybe excitement is on the way."

"Let's hope so."

The man who rode up so quickly was an army scout. He was out of breath, but managed to stammer out, "Colonel, it's Quanah Parker. I swear to God! He's coming in!"

"Quanah? How can you tell?"

"Well, he's riding a gray pony, and out of all the possible Comanche left on the plains, there's only one that sits a horse like this one. It's got to be Quanah."

Mackenzie felt his scalp prickle from the roots above his forehead all over his head and down the back of his neck. "How many are with him?"

"About ten braves, all unarmed. I reckon they've cached their weapons. A dozen old men, and maybe two or three dozen more younger women and children. Quanah's the only one on a horse. They all look like they came from hell."

"Let them come in unmolested. I'll receive them myself right down there. Bring a table and some chairs, Grayson."

"Aye, sir."

The Quohadi band lasted the winter on the high plains, afoot and almost without food. Several of the old ones had starved to death or coughed to death, mercifully before their starvation came. Quanah and his small band buried them all in the frozen earth. When spring came, only Quanah's band showed up at the hills of the blue flints.

The Great Spirit told him he was still the leader of his people, the eagle who must once more pluck the serpent from the earth. He must go where his people went, even if it meant walking the white man's road.

Quanah was dressed in full ceremonial buckskins, but not a single feather was in his hair. A lone eagle feather was tied to the mane of his horse. To those who understood the meaning of this at all, it signified much.

Behind him, as they neared the fort, grief began to overcome the women. They started to wail. The sounds were like red hot coals on Tonarcy's breaking heart and she, too, wailed. A brief command from Quanah silenced all of them. "We go as Quohadi, not weeping and howling like lost puppies."

Quanah's face became more set and stern as he neared the fort. Before he reached the gates, he slipped from his horse. As the bluecoats crowded around the opened gates and the parapets, and to their astonishment, he sent his horse running into the woods with a slap, its lone eagle feather lifted by the breeze. Quanah walked openhanded into the fort in peace.

He recognized Mackenzie, but did not speak to him. When Mackenzie spoke his name, a statement rather than a question, "Quanah," he briefly nodded his head. But his lips were sealed shut. That was the only word spoken.

Mackenzie sat staring into space. Here his enemy had walked into his camp and surrendered. Yet when Mackenzie looked into Quanah's eyes, he felt like the defeated one. Here was something unconquerable. He mused a bit further. No one else moved or spoke. Then Mackenzie spoke harshly and in anger, "Take them away. Pen them separately in quarantine for two weeks."

Quanah knew this was how it would be. Like cattle.

The army detachment closed about the small band of Comanches and led them away. Something in Quanah's face kept them from laying a hand on any of them.

Mackenzie got up from his chair, and suddenly felt tired and old. He walked into the telegraph office and asked the operator, "Do you still have that paper I typed up requesting a transfer?"

"Yes, sir."

"Send it."

As he walked back outside, he looked to where Quanah and his band were reaching the compound where the Comanches and Kiowas were settled. Grayson slid back alongside him, like an old dog or horse waiting to be petted.

"They'll be seeing him any moment."

"What of it?" Mackenzie wearily retorted.

In the compound now, there was a rustle of voices, like a small wind, then a few whoops and yells, then many cries all at once, like a thousand wild geese cooped up and suddenly set free. Grayson and Mackenzie listened intently, the small smile on Grayson's face vanishing when he glanced at Mackenzie.

The shouts grew louder. "Quanah! Quanah! Quanah! Quanah! Quanah!" Quanah, upon seeing his old friends, and learning they were still alive, answered back.

In the late evening sky, the dying sun grew red.

EPILOGUE

After Quanah led the last Comanches onto the reservation, the wars for the southern plains were over. That summer, Charles Goodnight drove a herd of cattle into the Palo Duro Canyon and claimed an empire.

Mackenzie's deed of slaying the horses will be argued as long as the story is told. He may have been right; the Comanches might have trailed him all night and restolen the horses. His command achieved the army objective: it drove the Comanches onto the reservation. Still, it is not something one can admire.

Mackenzie came out of the Civil War as one of the brightest stars in the army's firmament. Grant and others believed he would rise to the very top. Something about the Indian Wars changed him, however; bitterness ate a hole in his heart.

After he left Fort Sill, he chased the Apaches for another ten years among the barren rocks and mountains, and under the blistering sun of southern New Mexico. He began to drink heavily. Many stories are told about his end; he, too, became legendary. Some said he died a lonely alcoholic in a one-room adobe hut in New Mexico. Others say he was tied to a wagonwheel and horsewhipped by an angry barkeeper in San Antonio, and in the night, died of the whipping, his drunkenness, and exposure. Still others say his mind finally cracked and he was hauled east again, to waste away in an asylum for the insane.

There is probably some truth in all these stories. In any case, his glory was short-lived, though later, people ignorant of the facts would try to resurrect it. The Indian Wars defeated him and broke him. His life ended badly.

More could be written about Quanah's life after he led his people down the white man's road. He remained the great chief of the Comanches, and no one took his place when he died of old age in 1911.

He led his people till the last days. He went to Washington, and became a great friend of then Vice-President Teddy Roosevelt. He took Roosevelt and his rancher friends, Charles Goodnight and Lee Bivens, wolf hunting on the caprock. He bought a dozen buffalo from the Bronx Zoo and restocked the Wichita Mountains, where the herd still roams today.

He gained substantial lands for the Comanches in southwestern Oklahoma, and all his life kept the lands intact and owned in common by the whole tribe. For many years the area was called by the Comanches simply the Big Pasture.

He wisely let the traildrivers trail north across the Comanche grasslands but charged them a fee—several head on each occasion—and slowly built up a great cattle herd for his tribe. In this respect he outshone his friend, the legendary Goodnight, in that he ran more cattle on more land, and had more men obey him in friendship as well as tribal loyalty.

He saw the first railroad brought into western Oklahoma, and because of his financial backing, was named to its board of directors. Not all progress was kind to him. When he went with the great Kiowa chief, Satanta, to ride in the Fort Worth Fat Stock show, they stayed in one of the new hotels. Not knowing to turn off the new gas lamps, they blew them out. Satanta died of asphyxiation; Quanah, of stronger constitution, recovered, after he was pulled out of his room the next morning.

He converted to Christianity but kept his eight wives, fathering a total of twenty-seven children. He built a beautiful two-story frame house with stars on the roof, and a separate bedroom for each wife, though he always preferred to sleep in his tepee on the ground in back. It is said that when he rode his horse in Roosevelt's inaugural parade, his friend Teddy studiously advised him that his many wives were incompatible with Christianity. Teddy said something to the effect, "Why don't you pick out the best one and tell the rest to go away?" Quanah, after thinking a long moment, said, "You tell them."

Quanah continued the use of peyote. The Comanches, Kiowas, and other Oklahoma tribes formed the American Indian Church, to keep the peyote ritual and some of the old ways. As Quanah expressed it, "In too many of the white man's churches, the preacher goes in the church and talks *about* Jesus. With the help of Father Peyote, we go in and talk *to* Jesus."

The story has it that Quanah even taught the use of peyote to some European royalty. Suffice it to say that he never made a mystery of the use of peyote. The mysteries exist independently of man's help. Quanah believed that peyote only allowed one to more quickly enter the spirit world, to see the manifold connections as well as possibilities of all things.

Quanah harbored no bitterness toward white men as a group. Some of his daughters married white men, and yearly since his death, Quanah's descendants have gathered in Oklahoma or Texas in a family reunion, white and red alike.

Quanah often went to Washington to fight for the Comanches. He won for them enlargement of their lands and full American citizenship and voting rights. He also fought legal battles in Texas to remove his mother's bones to the Comanche reservation in Oklahoma, a task he eventually accomplished.

In short, he held the Comanche tribe together and carried it into the modern age. At last, being old and full of days, he died. He was buried alongside his mother near Cache, Oklahoma. At his request, these words were placed over his grave:

RESTING HERE UNTIL THE DAY
BREAKS AND THE SHADOWS FALL AWAY.
QUANAH PARKER
THE LAST CHIEF OF THE COMANCHES

THE RIVERS OF TEXAS

We crossed the wild Pecos, forded the Nueces,
Swum the Guadalupe, and followed the Brazos.
Red River runs thirsty, the Wichita clear.
Down by the Brazos I courted my dear.

> Sing lie, lie, lie, lee, lee, lee, give me your hand.
> Lie, lie, lie, lee, lee, lee, give me your hand.
> Lie, lie, lie, lee, lee, lee, give me your hand.
> There's many a river that waters the land.

The wild Angelina is glossy and gliding,
The crooked Colorado runs wicked and winding,
The old San Antonio, it crosses the plains,
But I never will walk by the Brazos again.

> Lie, lie, lie, lee, lee, lee, pole the boat on.
> Lie, lie, lie, lee, lee, lee, pole the boat on.
> Lie, lie, lie, lee, lee, lee, pole the boat on.
> My Brazos River sweetheart has left me and gone.

She kissed me, she hugged me, she called me her dandy.
The Trinity's muddy and the Brazos quicksandy.
She kissed me, she hugged me, she called me her own.
Down by the Brazos, she left me alone.

> Lie, lie, lie, lee, lee, lee, give me your hand.
> Lie, lie, lie, lee, lee, lee, give me your hand.
> Lie, lie, lie, lee, lee, lee, give me your hand.
> The Trinity's muddy, the Brazos quicksand.

The girls of Little River, they're plump and they're pretty.
The Sabine and Sulphur has many a beauty.
On the banks of the Neches, there's girls by the score.
Down by the Brazos, I'll wander no more.

> Lie, lie, lie, lee, lee, lee, give me your hand.
> Lie, lie, lie, lee, lee, lee, give me your hand.
> Lie, lie, lie, lee, lee, lee, give me your hand.
> There's many a river that waters the land.